1997

To Diana
With Love
Linda

AND AFTER THE RAIN...

Linda Machin

MINERVA PRESS
MONTREUX LONDON WASHINGTON

AND AFTER THE RAIN...
Copyright © Linda Machin 1997

ISBN 1 86106 097 1

First Published 1997 by
MINERVA PRESS
195 Knightsbridge
London SW7 1RE

Printed in Great Britain by
B.W.D Ltd, Northolt, Middlesex

AND AFTER THE RAIN...

Contents

Turkey and Mint Sauce

Joe was always boasting about his zany mother. She became something of a legend within his student circles. Joe did not suspect in the communal references to 'Maddy', short for Madeline and never called mother, that there was anything but pleasurable engagement with these maternal antics. From his boarding school days his mother had provided him with a fund of adventures with which to upstage the ordinariness of his contemporaries and their parents. Joe's relationship with his mother was almost totally second hand, that is to say that her taking care of him had never connected them, but her legendary life of travel and lovers and unconventionality drifted in clouds of extraordinariness to become a vicarious part of her son's experience. If he thought about it he had rarely shared in one of her adventures, only in its elaborate telling. His actual experience of his mother was much more about being told to stay quiet because she had a headache, or listening through the door to some noisy intimacy. Her friends and her lovers and even Joe's father danced attendance on this angel of mystery.

Just occasionally the fiction would touch reality and to Joe's delight he would be part of his mother's story. It was his fifteenth birthday and there was to be a weekend of celebrations including a fancy dress party. His school friends moved between real excitement at the possibility of meeting Joe's mother and an adolescent paralysis at the thought of some eventuality, for which no mental preparation was possible, which might humiliate their burgeoning sense of manhood. The days passed with plenty of fun but Dominic thought with irreverence that the only way that Maddy was different was that she behaved like his nineteen-year-old sister rather than his own reliable mother.

As the day of the fancy dress approached, speculation and intrigue abounded. Maddy hinted that she hadn't had much time to plan but her costume required the accompaniment of an animal. Alice and the white rabbit, Mary and a little lamb – the boys joked and let imagination run riot. Dominic could see how Maddy's reputation grew, she only had to throw down the gauntlet of intrigue or innuendo and everyone would go chasing after it. Reality was totally obscured by this mirage of fantasy and make believe.

When the hour of the party arrived the hesitant procession of pirates and Napoleons came from their rooms, filling the air with the hilarity of embarrassment rather than true enjoyment.

As each discovered the identity of the other Joe suddenly said, "Where's Maddy?"

"I saw her go out the back way," said cousin Delia, who, at twenty, found all this rather juvenile, but it was too much the social currency of their family for her to be able to do more than show a mild disinterest in the event. Joe rushed with his friends to the door and slowly out of the stable emerged his mother. A long fair wig covered her own immaculately coifed hair and fell around her naked body.

"Madeline," gasped Joe's father. Never had anyone – not even Joe – heard his mother called by her full name. Inscrutably she walked around the cobbled yard, the rhythm of her body movement echoing the slow clip-clop of the horse. The boys were transfixed – sometimes by the total sight of this graceful form on horseback, at others by the more particular awareness of her bare breasts. She slowly returned to the stable and the nonplussed boys went indoors. Masks and hats came off as the excited retelling of what they had just seen mingled with the delights of food and drink. Maddy never appeared at the party in person but that three or four minute overture was all that was necessary to give Joe a party never to be forgotten. The details of her appearance as Lady Godiva, embellished with fantasy and obscenity, made the telling as delightful, if not more so, as the experience.

The five years since that event had taken him into a new social world of students and a new audience for tales of Maddy. Like the rest Chris was intrigued. She had stepped from the world of her own hard-working parents and their aspirations for her success, based as much on a Maddy-like fantasy as on any real understanding of higher education. At times, though, she was irritated by Joe's stories, she wanted to defend her simple but loving mother, for not even the most out of the ordinary of her anecdotes could match those of Joe.

Joe would regale them, not for the first time, with the story of his mother's elegant plunge into the swimming pool at some high society cocktail party and of her drifting in chiffon with champagne, like the Lady of Shalott, down the pool as all watched in fear and admiration. The stories never seemed complete to Chris – surely the point at which she emerged bedraggled and cold was just as much part of the story – but they were always left, like some 1960s play, at a climax from which the voyeur must choose an ending. And somehow it would have been sacrilegious to even think of an ordinary ending for one of Maddy's escapades.

Chris thought of her own mother, moved up from assistant to floor manager at the DIY centre and her father, a welder at the local engineering firm. Stories of the boy who got his head stuck in a lavatory seat as his parents searched for the trappings of a new bathroom, or the 'initiation' of the work experience boys to the 'real world' by having their fly zips welded, somehow seemed so boring that Chris wondered how her sides could have ached and tears flowed when her parents had told such crass stories. Chris could feel her own ambivalence about Maddy creep into her consciousness; she was angry with the arrogance of Maddy's extroversion but she felt ripples of real delight at the way Maddy mocked the urbaneness of every day life. She somehow wished the solid goodness of her own mother could break resplendent onto the world's awareness like Maddy's did. She could not put her finger on the heroic qualities of her mother although they were there, whereas the candyfloss Maddy seemed always the heroine, but if you were to look deep it was only froth. Chris could not believe this unreal woman could prompt both the best and the worst feelings; certainly they were not feelings of indifference. Chris saw Joe not so much as a fellow student but as 'son of Maddy'; the spirit of his being was borrowed from the glamour of his mother. And yet the ambivalence she felt drew her to him and she seemed held as if by a spell. For his part Joe sensed an affinity with Chris that he indulged but did not analyse. He was a story teller not a philosopher; he observed or experienced life, he was not its commentator. Perhaps the yearning for a break from this tantalising umbilical tether with his mother lead him to the quiet warmth of Chris. She held no mystery but was uncomplicated, fun-loving and gentle.

"Would you like to come home for the weekend?" Joe asked Chris when their exams were over. "Maddy is doing an Australian 'Christmas'. She thought it would be fun to have all the trimmings in the sun instead of in cold December." Chris agreed, but wished she could be a fly on the wall rather than a real guest. Her quiet self-confidence was invaded with a sense of having none of the credentials for such an encounter with the unconventional.

The patio was resplendent with a trestle table of fine china and glass – rather French, Chris thought – and a Christmas tree with lights that hardly looked illuminated against the harshness of the sun. Maddy made a grand entrance in a chorus girl equivalent of a Father Christmas outfit. Everyone shrieked with laughter, but as the legend appeared Chris was suddenly consumed with a sickened sadness. The woman was pathetic, not funny, and as all around danced to her tune and to the making of another legend, Chris wanted to cry.

"Okay?" asked Joe, with a twinkle in his eye which sought Chris's approval for Maddy's mid-summer Christmas.

Chris nodded untruthfully and then asked,

"Do you love her?" Joe opened his mouth and closed it again. He had never ever considered the matter before and although the spontaneous answer should have been 'yes', the disarmingly straightforward Chris demanded the truth, and that would have been 'no'.

Instead Joe said, "She's not a conventional mother." Chris smiled.

The turkey sliced, Maddy, for the first time, noticed Chris and said,

"Can we pass you anything, dear?"

"Is there any mint sauce?" asked Chris. She saw instantly that her attempt to be as sophisticated and nonchalant as the famous Maddy had misfired.

"Mint sauce," Maddy mocked, and as always a cue from Maddy could never be ignored. Soon the whole table rocked to a chorus of disbelieving chortles, "Mint sauce."

"That goes with lamb," Joe whispered, embarrassed, to Chris.

"No it doesn't," said Chris, "it goes with anything you choose it to go with, in our house we even have it on bread for Sunday tea," she lied. No extravagance felt enough to match the fire of indignation she felt at this middle-aged phoney who could go naked before her son's friends and celebrate Christmas in June, and yet sneer at the perceived unconventionality of Chris's taste; it was unbearable!

Chris stood, confident with anger, "I can't possibly stay at such a dull gathering. To think that such a renowned social eccentric won't provide her guests with mint sauce to enhance their turkey!"

There was uncertainty as the company gauged whether Chris's declaration was made in jest or truth. No one had ever changed one of Maddy's social scripts; if they had it was only to ad lib and venerate her leading lady status to still greater heights.

"Do stay," said Maddy, shaken, and she rose slowly, champagne glass aloft, as if regaining an off-balance moment, only to emerge grander and more in charge. "Turkey and mint sauce," she said, as an elaborate toast to the unconventional.

"Turkey and mint sauce," they said in unison.

Triptych

I

"Meet my daughter Joanna," said Mrs Conolly to the consultant. "I thought it might be best if you met her rather than me. Joanna has been a tower of strength ever since Janet was born. I had my breakdown then and my health has been very fragile since. Joanna's love for me and Janet has been a constant source of encouragement, and even when I was at my most depressed, may I say, she loved me through it."

Jo had been introduced to numerous people over many years with little variation in this speech. For Jo it had the makings of the prologue of a Greek tragedy, or the introduction of a saint, but always it felt like an emotional trap from which she had never discovered an escape. That phrase 'she loved me through it' always had the same sickening feel for Jo. It wasn't that love had no meaning for her, but in her family it was the cloying currency of belonging. Whatever you felt, you had to engage in this prescribed way; it wasn't spontaneous care, it was dutifully imposed attachment. It had none of the joys that even the soppy and romantic fictional versions carried but rather a nauseating sweetness applied to a heavy, ensnaring way of being with each other.

Jo sought to put the record straight in a fashion that might not disturb her mother's illusions – it was too late for that – but would be seen by the consultant as nothing more than ordinary duty.

"I only did what anyone would have done in the circumstances."

"Always modest, my Joanna." Mrs Conolly took hold of Jo's hand and while Jo left it there physically, emotionally she snatched it back and in her head yelled, 'I hate this! I hate this! I hate this!'

"One thing is certain," said Dr Browning, not picking up the ambiguity, "Janet is going to need 'loving through' this stage of rehabilitation, or normalisation as we call it now. As I said to your mother on the phone, Joanna, our plans are to move Janet out of hospital and into some sheltered community housing. This hospital will be completely closed in the next four years. We have various workers in the community, nurses and social workers, who will settle her into this new lifestyle, but we need your help and, can I say, 'love' too." Jo froze inside, she could feel this nice patronising doctor using the same words to trap her as her mother had done. How could she say to this reasonable white-coated professional, 'I love Jan but even that is hard when it is forced into heavy responsibility – I love her for herself but I don't want to be responsible. The fact that love was demanded of me means it has been pressed and stifled into token loving'.

"Perhaps I should take you through the proposed steps."

"Could I suggest you talk this through with Joanna on her own," said Mrs Conolly. "I would be happier going for a cup of tea and leaving any decisions to her."

"That sounds like a good idea," said Dr Browning.

Jo sighed. Perhaps it was a good idea for a sweet, frail seventy year old to retreat to the WRVS booth, but she had done the same when Jan had been born and was diagnosed as suffering from Down's Syndrome. Jo had been fifteen and Mrs Conolly had been forty. Her father, she suspected, was shamed by this late pregnancy (was it even his? Jo couldn't begin to imagine her father's participation in her sister's conception with anything except incredulity and/or disgust) and with the even more shameful reality of a disabled daughter, he became more distant and engrossed in his work.

"Daddy is caring by providing," Mrs Conolly had said to her fifteen-year-old daughter, who, as an adolescent in the late fifties, carried the embarrassment first of a pregnant mother and then of a sister whose condition staunched the flow of all the usual baby curiosity and cooing. Just as Jo became more used to the reality a greater blow had followed; her mother had had a nervous breakdown and was kept in hospital for six months. The doctor said that the menopausal baby and its disability had been too much for her.

Mr Conolly had drawn his elder daughter on one side and said, "You are Janet's little mother now. Until Mummy is restored to us

Auntie Meg will have the baby in the day but you can look after her at
night and at the weekend. She needs your love, Joanna." There it
was again; what she now recognised as emotional blackmail, at fifteen
she only experienced as a resentment, for which she felt hugely guilty.
In the year of her O levels to be landed with such responsibility until
'Mummy is restored to us' and 'because she needs your love' was
unbearable.

In a strange sort of way Jo managed to work even more effectively
for her exams. The limited time was a wonderful and precious escape
from 'loving'. The routine was soon entrenched, with mother frail
and cosseted in her breakdown, father strong and absent in his earning
and Jo the loving little mother. What was worse than caring for Jan
(it had many compensations, she was content and cuddlesome and Jo
could share many of her feelings with the baby) was the weekly visit
to the hospital. The stereotyped images that were part of teenage
mythology about the madhouse seemed mild beside the bleak reality of
the Bastille-like buildings and strangely mad people. Oddly her
mother seemed like none of the other patients but had returned to a
pathetic child-like state of need. Jo's father punctuated the Sunday
afternoon visits with escapes to the garden to smoke, to have a word
with sister, to check the car was locked. His embarrassment was
transparent, but he was stoic in carrying the badge of 'love' for his
family; the campaign-like precision of delivering and collecting Jan to
and from his sister's, the weekly order of carnations for his wife, the
occasional chocolates to say thank you to Jo, and his relentless hard
work to give financial security.

Jo's aunt had once said in those early days, "Your father's a
brick." Jo knew what people meant by that, but she let her mind
meander over its more literal meaning and felt the truth of that too.
He was dutiful in his care of Jo, but there was no warmth; he was cold
and hard. Even her mother, pre-breakdown, offered only sugar-
coated duty, and Jo had never felt she could share things with her.
From her parents she received a mix of no emotion and pseudo-
emotion. It was all very confusing.

Mrs Conolly had in a very contrived way taken Jo on one side to
tell her the facts of life.

"You need to know about life and love." Her whispered and
breathless imparting of information (information for which Jo was
hungry, as she felt sure some of the anatomical facts she had so far

gleaned must be inaccurate) was as alien to the world either of them seemed to inhabit as would be the case had Mrs Conolly been describing a foreign custom in a foreign language. Mrs Conolly's desire to keep secret the fact of Jo's growing up from her father's knowledge or notice made Jo feel that they were involved in a conspiracy of which her father was totally innocent. It was in the context of this conversation that the word 'love' began to take on another meaning. It didn't have that public sense of saintly grandeur, previously implied by her mother, but rather a hushed and maybe devious meaning. Her mother talked of the 'love' of knowing a man in a faintly Old Testament way, but unlike the extravagant oozing of goodness that seemed to go with the other love, there was a tight-lipped resignation that indicated propriety not generosity. Jo was totally confused after the intimate session with her mother, not merely about some of the more mechanical elements of sexuality, but about adult relationships. All of the sniggering curiosity disappeared with the added mystery of her mother's late pregnancy. Jo was merely told by her mother that someone else would be coming to live with them. When Jo had wanted to pursue the details her mother had put her finger to her lips and pointed to her still trim stomach. Jo learned the exact truth via a friend whose mother had seen her mother at the hospital.

All these fragmented realities of loving came into Jo's head as she sat listening to the hospital plans for Jan. There was the same double meaning in all this too; it was for Janet's good – a new way of society showing a caring face, but then it would be cheaper than hospital, but resources might be 'a bit slim', to use Dr Browning's words, at the beginning. 'The hypocritical face of politics,' thought Jo.

Jo wanted to say, "And what has all this to do with me?" but instead she said, "How do you see the family helping with these plans?" Why was she so knotted up and subservient when in the other worlds she inhabited her strength and clarity were the hallmark of her talent?

Jo did love Jan. She had an ungainly woman's body and her clothes were ill-fitting and uncoordinated. Jo sometimes wondered if they did it on purpose to chide the patients for the inconvenience they caused. But in spite of all that, her demands for attention and giving of love were so simply expressed that sharing in it shed a refreshing perspective on the manipulative love her mother had squeezed from her over the years. Jan could laugh and skip, taking in the delights of a summer breeze and springy turf. Jo was quite relieved to enter Jan's world after the consultation with the doctor and the anxious prattle of her mother at the tea bar.

"I really think I shall have to leave it to you; since Daddy was taken from us I can't make decisions. I'm sure that doctor knows best, but I don't feel Janet will cope in a hostel. They can seem a bit harsh the nurses here, but underneath I know they really love their patients. Outside she wouldn't get that kind of love except from us, and I'm just a frail old woman now at the mercy of my ageing body." Jo felt the web of thirty years ago tighten around her. Her responsibility to show love was setting in motion a new programme of maternal control.

Jo returned with Jan to the day room to hear the doctor telling sister,

"Janet has a lovely family. It's a long time since I've seen such loving devotion. I think minimal community support will be necessary there."

If Jo had not come to know what real love was about she might have been fooled, but as it was she knew that she was dancing to the tune of so-called love, played to demand maximum responsibility and minimum warmth.

II

"Meet Mrs Stirling," Mike Dobson said to the visiting American.

"Oh! You're Max's wife. I'd heard a whisper that it was Dr not Mrs"

"No, she's plain Mrs as my wife, she's Dr with her maiden name." Max rushed from behind just in time to clear any misunderstanding about Jo's position.

"Jo Stirling, pleased to meet you," said Jo without a whisper of dissent from her husband's statement.

She looked attractive in the plain cream dress with the rather exotic earrings and necklace that Max had brought back from one of his trips to the Far East. Her even features, short dark hair and trim figure had always been a business asset for Max. As his father had pointed out many years earlier – 'You need a decorative wife to ease those tricky business deals'. Jo had always been that and she maintained an easy conversation with people without ever competing with Max.

He was a chauvinist, without doubt, but he had had enough that was genuine in him to woo Jo away from the prudish affectation of her parental home. They had met via another boyfriend of Jo's. When she had been a student, theirs had been a fairly straightforward relationship in which Jo neither colluded with or challenged Max's chauvinism. It wasn't even called that when she was a student, and his handsome, easy popularity felt like a forceful antidote to the self-conscious and prissy ways of the Conollys. He had had money, even then, and the budding entrepreneur could beat student hospitality any day. It wasn't that Jo was looking for a generous he-man, though many of her friends were, but simply that nothing seemed to stop the progression of their relationship from dates to marriage.

Max always disassociated himself from Jo's academic pursuits and the socialising that went with them. At first he would excuse himself from meeting with her friends on account of some pressing business arrangement, but later she neither troubled to invite him nor he to find an excuse; they were two different worlds. Similarly, with her family he paid the minimum of dutiful visits, and inquired when appropriate, but left the caring bit to Jo. At least this latter role fitted more snugly into his view of the 'little woman'. Jo cringed when she recognised in such phrases the sexist perspective that was Max and she learnt later to challenge his language so that he was not an irritation or embarrassment to her, even though he couldn't quite see what all the fuss was about.

Many times Jo stopped to reflect on her marriage and the incongruities within their relationship, but it worked well enough and had reached the point where they had been together long enough to have the stability of a shared history and the comforts of familiarity in day to day life.

Not that much of their day to day life coincided; each had demanding commitments which took them separate ways. It might have been different had their been children, but after the miscarriage Jo had retreated from the possibilities of motherhood as one relieved to have had a near miss. Max would have liked children, perhaps more as a sign of his virility than out of a strong paternal desire, but after losing the baby it wasn't a high priority and was excluded from their agenda. Yes, agenda was how it was. They fell into a routine in

which even love making had to be fitted in alongside making money
and moving up the career ladder. Only childless couples desperate to
make a child are as calculated and contrived about their love making
as Jo and Max.

'What happens if I come back overnight from that Institute
conference and you delay seeing your mother until Saturday – we
could have a night of passion next week.' You would think booking it
in their diaries would rob it of all spontaneity, but no, they would
come together with the physical energy of new lovers. At least that's
how it was for Max; the physical momentum of his love, or more
usually lust, was often a replay of all those Rugby Club tales and
changing room discussions. For Jo this seemed much healthier than
the puritanical games (if puritans even played games) which she
imagined her parents had played. It was honest, undisguised sexuality
which, while not truly satisfying to her, seemed as much as could be
hoped for. She was satisfyingly functional, as far as she could see
when she looked at the baby-like relaxation in Max's face as he slept a
deep and peaceful sleep after making love. It was only with the
arrival of Nick that she was confronted with the years of perfunctory
and unsatisfactory sex which she had endured. Part of her long
suffering, it has to be said, was about disinterest too. She had learned
from an early age that if life is a bore, or unfair, at least in your head
you can be somewhere else. For Jo it was not so much lying back and
thinking of England, as plotting the next steps in her research scheme.

Jo and Max were conventional in their unconventionality. Jo's
place in this part of her life did depend upon being one step behind
and below Max except in the traditions of home making. Jo had a
flair – whether she would have, had she not been married to a well-
heeled business man is another matter – for interior design and cordon
bleu cookery. Max entertained with style and Jo was the ideal partner
to show off the fruits of his success in soundly excellent rather than
lavish ways.

"Perhaps we could have a little supper party for the two Americans
and their wives and Mike Dobson and his wife." Max planned for
such events and had a superb knack of infusing the precision and
formality of arrangements with an easy informality. Part of it was
Jo's skill too, but Max would never recognise that, she merely
cooperated with his careful planning, He would decide the menu and
only if the butcher let them down with a less than perfect piece of

meat would he say to Jo, "There, I shouldn't have been persuaded by you, we should have had lamb not beef." Had it mattered to Jo she might have protested, but all of this was a much smaller part of her life than it was of Max's, so why make him unhappy by arguing.

"Try the vol-au-vent, it's Jo's speciality," said Max excitedly to one of the Americans. "Yes she got that picture at a London saleroom. It cost the earth but it's wonderful on that wall."

It was only with the arrival of Nick that Jo suddenly saw that what passed as a compliment to her was all part of Max controlling their social world; keeping her within the prescribed limits of housewifery was no longer a subtle form of his sexism. What had passed for so many years as comfort and a sustaining relationship began to jar, and Jo saw that, for Max, she was little more than an *objet d'art* – pleasing to look at, creative, and a servant of his materialistic world. Jo did not know what to do with this realisation and she wondered whether she had been happier as a naïve pawn in Max's game. But, like knowledge which cannot be unlearned, the insights into the exploitative nature of her marriage filled her with fury.

Max thought it was a new middle-aged game Jo was playing, so that her resistance to sex was, as he saw it, a teasing gesture for him to persist. On several occasions his persistence moved into violence and both were shaken by his unstoppable aggression. Max hadn't time to regard it as any more than a menopausal whim of Jo's. However, Jo knew that whatever the world might see in their marriage, the physical and materialistic realities which had cemented their union for twenty odd years were coming unstuck. Jo felt trapped. The lifestyle with Max was so much part of her, it had helped relieve the years of anguish with her mother and Jan and was a wonderful contrast to the intensity of her academic pursuits; letting it go seemed impossible.

"Mrs Stirling has won the first class pastry prize at the village show for the last six years," said Mike Dobson's wife to the portly American. 'The pastry prize' Jo scoffed in her own head at the triviality of such conversation. But this was a habitation of contracts, cars, cash cards, caviar and coitus; no emotion tempered the robotic games which ran to the patterned time of computer phonics. 'Even a bit of guilt might make it all human', thought Jo, 'a world of things and doing, but no heart, that's Max and me.'

III

"Meet Dr Conolly," said Jo's boss, Douglas Walters.

"Pleased to meet you, Dr Conolly, I can't wait to talk about your recent findings in more detail. The papers you sent were fascinating."

"My pleasure," said Jo, "I hardly dare believe we've made a break through, but it is just possible."

"Dr Conolly's a scientist at heart, Professor Blake, that's why she keeps a dispassionate scepticism even about her own work."

The two men laughed and Jo smiled uncomfortably. She was twitchy about this meeting and almost felt wrong-footed by Douglas, who was presuming to unveil his protégé by revealing what lay at her heart. It hardly mattered but somehow it felt like a subtle academic version of Max's sexism, in which words map out territory and ownership of women. She realised that she was being touchy, but she'd spent the night with Nick and somehow she thought only he had the right to say what lay in her heart.

This dizzy little internal dialogue ceased as they reached Jo's room. It was a busy work place with books and papers, but odd hints of its female resident singled it out from other colleagues' rooms; there was a carefully-watered sill full of plants, not just dried up spider plants but mature flowering plants all complementing each other and arranged in appropriate relationship to each other. Two Rodin nudes tastefully framed, and an oriental-looking jar of pot pourri were further clues to the gender and good taste of the occupant.

"Come in, Professor Blake, perhaps I could begin by showing you some of the data we're analysing before we go to the results."

"Certainly, it would help to grasp the background to your work."

Jo moved about the documents with total ease and an unselfconsciousness that was infectious to her watching colleagues. They had shared in parts of her work, but watching Jo captain her own enterprise was fascinating.

Jo began her career in medicine but quickly showed a flair for pathology. Her student friends were quick to point out that she was best with dead patients. The truth was she was better at true scientific investigation than she was at doing detective work from the uncertain base of patients' own descriptions of their symptoms. She liked the patients and got on with them but as a doctor she was frustrated. She told her disappointed parents, who had seen their daughter as a medical saviour loved by thousands of grateful patients, that she could be a nurse or a pathologist but not a doctor. Given that the choice was not theirs anyway she decided to specialise in the area of medicine which seemed to beckon her.

Ironically, the breakthrough, which Jo now seemed on the brink of making, would cause thousands to be grateful to her, but she would never have that personal affirming exchange with them for which her parents so yearned. Jo was beginning to isolate some carcinogenic elements in food processing and connect them with vulnerable host conditions. There had been years of painstaking data collection, processing, and correlating, and now some of this was coming to an exciting conclusion. Prof. Blake from the States had begun finding something similar a year ago but premature publicity had blocked some of the areas of investigation – vested business interest closed ranks on research which might be financially damaging.

Jo could feel the words and ideas tumble from her as she talked about the research. It was as if her brain were a separate agent of activity and communication and once plugged in could offer thoughts at a rate equivalent to any computer printout. Both to herself and her colleagues, at times like this, her brilliance rendered her genderless – she was a hugely talented human being. Douglas' inclination to patronise or put her down was swamped by his own engagement with her mental output. At times it was difficult for them to keep up. That was partly because she was articulate and partly because of the depth at which she had absorbed and understood her own work over many years. Douglas looked at his watch.

"I think we should break for lunch. Our brains need rest and nourishment."

Jo walked over to the refectory with Prof. Blake. It was difficult for her to cease the flow once begun, and the interruption in her explanations left her strangely ill at ease with everyday chat. Inside, a sense of alarm gripped her. If this had been one of Max's social do's she would have had a perfect range of topics to dip into and tease out. What was different? She wondered whether as a woman she couldn't sustain her own brilliance and was curiously returned, like Cinderella at midnight, to a pumpkin-like state of normality in which women do not glow with a full range of competence and glory.

'What nonsense,' she thought, and conscious of changing gear on a steep gradient, said to Prof. Blake – "Are you familiar with the architectural and art treasures of Cambridge?"

Thankfully another element of her intellectual capacity came to her and once again her striking, maverick mind flashed dozens of pieces of knowledge and fascinatingly juxtaposed ideas before her colleagues. The lunch proved as intellectually scintillating as the morning had done and Jo had that familiar feeling which comes from having used a lot of mental energy, when even more energy, often of a superior quality, is generated. In another context it might be described as 'getting high' but in this context it was the stuff of academic exchange and the seed-bed of innovative thinking.

Prof. Blake had several days in Cambridge and a number of meetings were fixed for his collaboration with Jo to be formalised.

"You must come to the States. That seems like the only way we can put our work together."

For the first time Jo was conscious of other life influences and hesitated.

"That might be difficult," she said.

"Possessive husband," grinned the Professor.

"No, certainly not, I wouldn't let him be," said Jo in an indignant mood. Prof. Blake knew he'd got that one wrong.

"We'll have a look at your work schedule and we'll see what can be done. I really do think it's imperative that you come."

"I'll see what's possible," said Jo.

She returned to an empty house that night; Max was in Sweden. It was the strange and dutiful pull of her mother's needs and the strong and undutiful pull of Nick which were exercising her heart and mind. Was this really being the liberated, intellectual woman? She couldn't decide, but instead dipped into the briefcase full of journals that awaited her attention. A conference paper presented at Yale caught her eye. 'The role of women in scientific discovery – what part does gender play in the pursuit of excellence?' Jo sat back and enjoyed the affirmation of female intellect and knew that she was playing her part; it was something to be prized. Her pride was flourishing – the phone rang.

It was Douglas Walters.

"It's important for you and the department that you take up the offer to go to the States. Nothing must stand in the way of this wonderful opportunity." Jo made no response, Douglas continued "I assume your silence is assent, anything else would be impossible; I'll see you tomorrow and we'll set it all in motion."

Jo sat in silence. the brain that served her so well was switched off, only the beating of her heart and her shaky hand registered the human response to the glittering prize.

Post Script

Jo lay in the warm sun. Nick had gone back in to fetch a drink while they awaited their ploughman's lunch. She stretched in contentment, savouring this bit of unscripted living. Here was a world where roles and responsibilities did not exist and she was known as herself. The cost of such luxury was secrecy; if it didn't fit with the rules or the rules couldn't be made to fit it, then it was outlawed. She and Nick had been lovers now for three years. There was pain and frustration but that was nothing when set in the context of their loving. It had a bitter-sweetness about it, the hurting and yet the beauty of what they shared together.

This was a whole day just for them, before Nick went off to Europe for a two week concert tour. Jo had caught the stopping train out of Cambridge and Nick had met her at Waterbeach. It was all part of avoiding people they knew. They set off without plans; being with each other was enough. Events and anecdotes tripped and danced between them as they laughed with a heady pleasure that covered what they knew would soon be another goodbye.

It was already two o'clock when they decided to stop at an inviting pub by the river for lunch. The harassed barmaid informed them lunch was finished, and the messy tables laden with the debris of other people's eating reinforced her unobliging response.

"Perhaps a sandwich," said Nick with the sort of optimism that cannot be thwarted.

"Okay," said the tired and probably off-duty barmaid. "Will a ploughman's do you?" Jo giggled at her use of the phrase, knowing that it was probably less trouble to throw a pickle and some cheese onto a plate than it was to make a sandwich. "In or out?" she inquired, with an economy of words that hinted at her unappreciated and exhausted state.

"Out," said Nick, "if that's not too much trouble. You look as if you could do with a rest and some refreshment yourself. Busy spot this." The latter phrase could be taken as a statement or a question depending on what energy the girl had to respond. She smiled, a tired but appreciative warmth lit the weary face and she disappeared.

Nick led Jo into the garden. They decided to sit on the grass rather than make space amongst the dishes. It felt like a space that had been noisily peopled but now only bore the still-life scars of the joviality and perhaps vulgarity of passing travellers.

They sat quietly; a quiet not as a vacuum but as a vibrant and still communication between them. The passing glance of their eyes lingered for moments of deep soul communion.

"I love you", said Jo, breaking the silence, "and I'm very thirsty."

Nick jumped to his feet and laughed – "I should have remembered your other appetites."

Jo felt the slight dampness in the grass beneath her but it gave a coolness in contrast to the heat of the July sun. The domestic clatter from the pub kitchen became obscured in her awareness, and was replaced by the sounds of the river bank. Jo knew that it was being with Nick that had liberated her attention for the natural world. Just being with him was more powerful than working with a team of her intellectually charismatic colleagues. He touched a nerve which opened a door to her soul.

Jo was afraid to confine her mental reflections upon their relationship to a catalogue of meetings and dates and times, for fear that a mere logging of their lives together would rob it of the mystical spontaneity that gave her back her self. She wanted to capture the richness of experience as well as the shape of events. Her mind and emotions delved amongst the treasures of their loving. Their meetings were often opportunistic rather than planned. 'I've got an hour, meet me for lunch,' or 'The rehearsal's off – Jane has flu and Gerry missed the train – we could have the flat to ourselves for a couple of hours.' Jo learned to be flexible, knowing that even if she left in the middle of a piece of work she would still complete it on time. Sometimes these unexpected meetings felt romantic, at others the sheer uncertainty made her moody and angry. But whatever resentment she took in her heart, it melted when she was with Nick.

The way they were together had an integrated 'rightness' about it. In the early days she had wondered whether it was just sexual attraction, but she always knew when they made love that it was an expression of something much deeper than physical desire. She guessed that in part it had something to do with Nick being a musician. He had the capacity to make love in the way, she imagined, he must make music, giving completely of himself and yet, within that act of total giving, receiving back with orgasmic delight the shared expression of harmony and joy. She never felt functional or humanly incidental but at the centre of a mutual and passionate act of discovery and creativity. They would take turns in initiating love, but then each knew how to make it a totally fulfilling experience for the other. Their touching, too, had a quality of testing out what was lying hidden in the heart. The awareness of hands held over a snatched drink might invite 'What sadness hides behind that smile,' or 'I know there aren't words when you're hurting, just let me hold some of the pain.' It was as if their repertoire of communication was so wide that at times words had no place, at others articulations sprang from a poetic depth that reflected their inner hearts.

It was hard to know what would come of their relationship. Trying to fit it into the normal social shape of human relationships robbed it of the vibrant life that it possessed and demonstrated. Relaxed in the reality of this immense loving Jo felt completely the person she knew that she was and wanted to be.

She heard Nick's voice, "You must come over and meet her."

"Meet Dave," said Nick, "he'll probably replace Rob in the quartet when he goes to New York in the autumn. He's just stopped for a quick drink en route to meet his wife in Norwich."

"Good to meet you," said Dave, looking Jo fully in the eye, "I know now what is the source of life's sparkle for Nick – besides Mozart and Hadyn."

Jo, knowing the reality of their love was visible, dared to believe this was where she belonged. Her body and mind and spirit were for this moment limited and centred.

When Dave had gone they sat silent and contemplative, eating their lunch and moving in and out of their separate reveries and into that quiet touching of hearts.

Jo held Nick's hand, "At last I know me," she said, "thanks to your love,"

For the moment, what lay beyond this immediate horizon was unclear and did not matter.

Stroke

"It's hard to tell how much functioning will be restored but it looks to be quite a severe stoke," said the ward sister to Christine.

In response to Don's watery and vacant eye Christine cast a disdainful look, and within his staggering brain function he saw the sneering, dismissive look his mother gave him, 'snivelling child,' she would say, 'get out of my sight.' It was there he recognised it, in his heart and in the guttering spasms of his mind. A drowning man is said to have his life flash before him and for Don the pained expression on his daughter's face brought connecting memories of the past before him with kaleidoscopic clarity.

"I'm not sure how much he understands," resumed the sister, "but I'm sure it will help if you could spend a little time with him. Were you planning on staying for a few days?"

"I will have to be guided by things at work," said Christine, eager not to make a premature trap for herself but wanting to appease the guilt she felt for all the bureaucratic energy which had gone into tracking her down. While the alienation from her father was a private matter, she could handle it, but once consultants and record clerks and police officers and local radio stations were involved in reuniting her with her father the cluster of feelings that moved between embarrassment and danger, and guilt and pity and self-pity were caught in a knot of physical discomfort that she desperately wanted to cast off. One way was to be seen to do her 'duty' but the ambivalence in their relationship made this no easy strategy to fathom out.

"Obviously I'll also be guided by you," she said as a kind of afterthought, but knew that on both occasions she had used the word 'guide' judiciously, as a way of leaving her own ultimate right to decide intact. "I'll sit with him for a little while," she said, as if to terminate the discussion with the ward sister.

"That's fine, we're busy keeping a close eye on him, but you're welcome to stay as long as you like."

Christine felt a sense of irritation at the mixed messages – she was needed, urgently, but the sister's words, far from reassuring her of 'welcome', merely reinforced the sense she always had in hospitals that relatives only have a place if they are administered in prescribed doses by staff, expert and wise, in all things human.

"I'll not get in the way," she replied, as if to play her part in the power game by decoding the sister's cryptic message.

Don had drifted from the present, and the voices by his bed were distant realities compared with the sounds and sights which filled his head. His solitary childhood had been full of anguish – a pain which was so enormous he didn't know how to handle it. The spilling of his pain had incurred the further wrath of his mother who despised her weakling son. She was a large, hard-working, bad-tempered woman married to an equally large, hard-working, bad-tempered man. Don could never imagine what had brought them together and it was only when his mother died, apparently of grief, within weeks of his father's death that he saw what, for most people, would be the currency of destruction, was a strange kind of creative connection for his parents. Their sparring, though obviously a vibrant necessity for them, was for Don a deadly battlefield in which the fantasy of his own abandonment (in the event of a split surely neither parent would want the irksome responsibility of this weedy, simpering child) featured as large and real as the verbal and physical ricochet of blows that flew between them. Sometimes they locked him in his room, he assumed as punishment for some unknown crime he had committed, but later he saw that it was to remove a distracting factor from the battlefield. Strangely, while he mentally deduced it to be a punishment, emotionally he experienced it as release into a haven, unassailed by events over which he had no control. It did not matter that the key was on the other side. He knew that in an hour or two his mother would turn it and in an aggressive way abuse him for staying in his room. Even little Don dismissed this part of the drama as a game, blaming neither himself for not escaping captivity, nor her for the unreasonableness of her expectation.

Don had few aspirations for his future. How could he when plied with endless messages about his stupidity, weakness, idleness? He saw himself as the hopeless creature described ceaselessly to him by his parents. Even following his father's footsteps into the mine, was described as a job too good for him – man's work not woman's. Working in the pit was a disaster. All the sneering he suffered at his father's hand was multiplied by his father's cronies. Don didn't altogether recognise it as part of the banter between the different generations of miners and that, for many, the quips came with a rough sort of kindness, that was outside his experience. It was all indistinguishable from the spiteful jests made at home.

How two such bullies could create a child with any sensitivity was a mystery and certainly most of Don's gentle responsiveness lay dormant until much later, but it did begin to show with his love of the countryside. Perhaps because it represented escape from the people and the confines of the pit and the oppressive bleakness of a working class house, he relished the Sunday afternoon walks. For the first mile or two the vegetation had a dusty veneer of grime that masked the freshness of green things. But if he walked far enough the bird calls seemed clearer, the hedgerows were more colourful and freer and Don began to detect a range of feelings quite unlike any he had previously experienced. There was a physical lightness and warmth that must, he thought one day, be what happiness is. He knew that these excursions would be mocked if his parents knew about them but their own preoccupations, and general disinterest in a twenty-year-old 'failed' son, robbed them of any curiosity about these absences on Sunday afternoon.

On one such ramble he met Stan, fishing. Stan worked down the pit and his red hair and freckled face were the butt of many a joke. They never became close enough to be regarded as mates but Don always felt an affinity with Stan. Stan was a fund of information about wildlife along the river bank. His usual intense and worried expression was transformed into that of an animated commentator on plant, animal and bird life. For the first time in his life Don knew what it was to admire someone and to desire knowledge. Nothing in his home, school or work life had ever inspired him with such a notion. These two young men, marginalised in the affairs of working-class culture, flourished in their outdoor relationship, sparring for knowledge and discovery, in a way which caused each to blossom.

"Come back for tea," said Stan one Sunday to Don. A momentary cloud passed over Don's face as his mind processed the awful possibility that the freeing relationship he had with Stan would be defiled or diluted by taking it back into their everyday worlds. The cloud cleared; perhaps it was a widening opportunity, not a restrictive one.

"Yes, great, I'd love to ."

Stan's house was in every way a replica of Don's; a terraced house pushed and cajoled into a narrow, high, dark wedge of living space, whose contents were drab and spartan. Though the physical differences were negligible – the beige curtains had a different pattern, Stan's mother had plates on the outside of the dresser while Don's mother had them stacked inside, plants struggling for survival in the claustrophobic atmosphere of banked-up fires were placed on different pieces of receptive furniture – the atmospheric realities of Stan's house were a world apart from Don's.

"Come in, Don," said Stan's mother, "we've heard a lot about you. I've kept asking Stan to bring you home but he knew you were a bit shy. Anyway make yourself at home." Don had heard this latter phrase before but was mystified as to its meaning. It sounded like a good thing to make yourself, but home for him lacked any of the experiences that would suggest comfort, either physical or emotional. "Meet Dora," Stan's mother said, "she's a bit shy too, but she's a good girl," She said this fondly and Dora smiled coyly with downcast eyes.

The tea was delicious – egg sandwiches and Madeira cake. The Jenkins infused the meal with a sense of occasion, and yet ease, that pulsed around Don like the ripples from a warm bath. He was to have that feeling again many times – at Christmas when the family meal was more than the special extras that loaded the table, when he lay in the sun on his first visit to the seaside – but every time he remembered that first Sunday tea at the Jenkins' as a true marker in his history.

The friendship with Stan was always special but it lead on to two other very significant life changes for Don. First, a chance to move from the pit to be a portering 'dogsbody' at the local station, under the watchful eye of Mr Jenkins the station master, and second, to marrying Dora.

These two events collapsed into a muddled memory that Don could only snatch at with his stroke-damaged mind. Disconnected phrases and pictures joined these important parts of his history into a meagre patchwork of autobiographical happenings. He saw in his head Millside station and recaptured the excitement that went with the arrival and departure of trains, mailbags, milk churns, trucks, tearful partings made mysterious by the steamy exhalations of the stationary train, happy meetings, sad meetings, cold hands around mugs of tea in winter, trowel-tickled flower beds in summer. Don had been happy. The freedoms and the responsibilities had liberated a sense of purpose that would have seemed quite improbable a few years earlier. Even his parents mellowed slightly, 'having a son in uniform', but it never gave way to any sustained encouragement, merely a passing reference to Don's rise in the world.

And Dora, she was a gem. Even now, Don could see her on their wedding day – an embarrassing occasion when even the warm generosity of the Jenkins household froze slightly with Don's parents' uncouthness and vulgarity. Don was ashamed, but society dictated that at least on this occasion there should be a meeting of kin. Thankfully it never happened again. But Don's happiness could not be dampened, and finding the gently subservient Dora as his wife was beyond all belief.

The routines of their married life owed more to the Jenkins' lifestyle than to the Morrisons', but, Dora having set the scene, Don quickly took up the cues and was master in his own house. A house that went with the job and was a slightly more modern version of all the homes they knew.

Don's weary eyes flickered as he concentrated his memory on the living-room of their station cottage. He roamed among the long-forgotten but now clearly-pictured furnishings, and alighted on the wireless. Don was not one for extravagance, in fact the multidimensional poverty of his youth induced a meanness that was sometimes difficult for Dora and always difficult for Christine. The wireless had been his extravagance. He had saved for the most expensive one available: a high-domed wooden one like a model cathedral which was given pride of place in their living-room. Don would ceremonially switch it on when their evening meal was cleared away and Dora got out her knitting. No one else was allowed to touch it, except of course for Dora to dust it every day. Long after it had ceased to function and Don had a little transistor, the old vehicle of sound transmission, ugly to Christine, beautiful to Don, was kept visually central.

Christine looked down at Don as he sighed heavily. She was unsure whether this exhalation warranted medical interpretation or whether it signalled the punctuated contemplative silence that had so irritated her as a child. Don's eyes moved slowly and looked in an unfocussed, dazed fashion on Christine. It made her feel very uncomfortable. It made him feel uncomfortable.

His mind again leapt into fleeting snapshot images of the past. His happiness with Dora, made complete, or so he had thought, with the birth of a daughter. But no, he felt that all her gentler characteristics were totally swamped by the thrusting, angry energies which she seemed to have inherited from his parents. Dora mocked his paranoia and said that their naturally intelligent and spirited child was an expression of herself and not a visitation from an earlier generation. Don did not see this and whether it was the extravagant tantrum of three-year-old Christine, the ten-year-old panting defiance or the teenager set to make her own rules, he would proclaim, 'that's a bit of her granny Morrison and I won't have it.' Don and Christine battled, not with the unseemly physical and verbal haranguing he had observed as a child, but an insidious and vicious meanness grew between them. What had cemented his parents marriage seemed to create a rift between Don and his daughter. It became a great grief for Dora as she ineffectively sought to reconcile them. Christine was bright and won a scholarship to university. Her sharper intellect in scything down Don's inarticulate protestations only served to harden his heart against her.

Two sprightly young nurses were making the bed next to Don's. Christine speculated, in her anxious boredom, whether the earlier occupant had been discharged or died. With Sister occupied behind curtains down the ward, the nurses used this patient-less piece of occupation to tease and joke and skip around the bed. Sheets were swung aloft with extravagant flourishes and allowed to billow out onto the waiting mattress. It dropped and they snatched the white starched linen to have a second giggling shot at the target. This time they jointly thwacked the sheet against the hard, plastic mattress.

The strident sound caused Don's mind to stand still in tremulous fear, and then it began to open to the cause of that fear. Christine had been especially rebellious at fourteen. Don had felt a new powerlessness in the face of her burgeoning womanhood, and felt sure that he must maintain some mastery of the situation if he and Dora were not to have shame brought on them by their daughter. They had been over to Stan's for tea one Saturday and returned to find Christine recumbent on the sofa with a young man. Both were red faced and panting – a posture quickly echoed by Don.

"Get upstairs young lady," he screamed "and as for you, young man, I don't ever want to set eyes on you again."

The rage he felt must have been inherited from his parents, but until that day it had lain dormant. Christine fled to her room screeching the innocence of their activity while the livid Don moved two stairs at a time to her room. She lay sobbing with anger and not remorse. Don took his leather belt and thwacked it down on the bed (had he not heard the noise a moment ago?). The vehemence of his temper accelerated as the cruel words of abuse spilled from him and he lashed out with his belt over and over again against the end of the bed. The movement of his arm seemed to gain a momentum of its own as the emotions and the words fuelled a frightening fury within him. Suddenly he became aware that Christine's screams were not of defiance but of pain and he stopped in paralysed disgust as he saw the reddened weals on her cheek and legs. The thrashing onto the bed had become a vicious stroke of the belt against Christine's young flesh. Dora stood at the door and wept bitterly – for her hurt child, for her cruel husband and for herself as victim of their senseless hate.

After that all matters relating to Christine were handled by Dora. His surly withdrawal attributed all wrong to Christine and he seemed to blot out the damage of his actions. For her part she was happy to glide into independence without deference to the man who had abused her with the stroke of his belt. Yes, abuse was the term, it was no use denying what that vicious stroke had been. She would not at the time have used the word with reference to that angry attack, but the feelings had hardened with the years, especially since her mother's death, and it served her own fantasies of hurt emotions to see her father as an abuser. The cracking noise of the sheet on the bed had jerked Christine too into a memory of that awful night. She looked down at the sunken face of this old man. As a little girl had she not been proud of her uniformed father when she compared him with the heavy-booted feet and coal-rimmed eyes of the collier fathers of her friends? But somehow he always wanted to do battle, often over things that didn't matter to Christine, but she couldn't bear to see him win so she would go on picking a fight for the sake of it.

The tired body shifted heavily and Don looked up, this time apparently with perfect focus.

"I'm, I'm..." The words were lost in the spittle and immobile lips. Christine felt the discomfort of not knowing what to do either to liberate the wordless groaning of her father or to relieve her own confused distress. She thought she would have more compassion for a stranger than for this sick old man who had marked her growing with a savagery that could still make her afraid.

"He was trying to say something," said Christine to the sister.

"Let's have a look at you, Donald," she said in that authoritarian and patronising way that nurses use most easily to relate to their patients. "I think he needs some sleep," she said, almost as if to accuse Christine of keeping him awake.

"I'll go and come back this evening," Christine said.

"It's hard to see someone you love suffering." Given the circumstances, this insensitive sensitivity dealt Christine a blow which spontaneously produced tears as surely as it would had the blow been one between the eyes.

"There there," said the sister, anxious not to incur another casualty on her already busy ward.

"It's okay," said Christine. "It's just that life hurts a lot and I feel quite emotional." She had come resentful and hating and now she just felt empty and sad. Her own head had been full of memories as she sat abstractedly with Don, but strangely there had been moments when a flickering connection had come between them. Christine rose from the chair, stiff with immobility and the concentrated replay of her life.

"I'm sorry," she said aloud. Her words slipped out like a reflex, it wasn't sorrow for anything in particular or sorrow that came as a calculated apology. In fact there were things for which she righteously felt she was owed an apology and yet she leant closely to the old man's ear. "I'm sorry," she said.

He struggled pitifully to gain mastery over his uncontrolled body; a stammering stream of sounds betokened huge mental energy. There was no sense to be made of it except, within this muddled outpouring, Christine felt sure, he said "Me too." She caressed his twitching hand and left.

The Dinner Party

Kate stood back from the table to check she had missed nothing. She had the clever knack when giving dinner parties of combining precision with a casualness, which deceived her guests as to the time and energy put into it, so conveying a relaxed welcome to them. It came partly from her student days in the sixties when she threw off the suburban mantle of her mother. Mrs Bartholomew entertained infrequently but when she did, it was an unbearable exercise of mounting tension in which pleasure decreased in proportion to the climax of food preparation, house cleaning and guest arrival. By the time all was in place, physical and emotional energy were so depleted that no one enjoyed their time together. From an early age, Kate realised that her mother had no friends, certainly not a best friend like Amy was to Kate. It was as if the public face of her mother was so denuded of life and warmth that people tiptoed around her, making the odd gesture that reminded Kate that she was a person not an object.

Kate seldom received any warmth from her mother, who took parenting, like entertaining, so seriously, that unless she had double checked her strategy with Dr Spock she hesitated to commit herself to any of Kate's needs. Just occasionally she could recall a moment's real contact which was so rare that Kate hardly believed it had happened. On one such occasion, Kate, as a headstrong five year old, had dashed in front of a car as she was coming home from school. Her mother had spontaneously taken the shaken, surprised child in her arms and rocked her gently, smoothing her hair and spilling warm tears onto her head as she said,

"I love you, I love you, darling Kate I couldn't bear for anything to happen to you." Never before or since had she received such words that clearly came from her mother's heart. For a long time it gave Kate a kind of childish status and joy and she felt a superior sense of connection with her mother; holding her hand in a way that

clearly embarrassed her mother, but which seemed totally at one to
Kate, with the wonderful declaration of love she had so recently
received from her. By the time she went to university any such sense
of connection with her mother had been eroded by years of formality
and living by a rigid script. It was justified by some code of
correctness which was pseudo-religious but lacking in any of the
ethics or mysticism which might go with religion.

Kate did not consciously reject all of her own history and the
models for living offered by her mother, but somehow an emotional
and social polarity resulted in Kate being a totally opposite kind of
person to her mother. Evenings were spent with friends with endless
mugs of coffee – no saucers, no mats, no finesse – but lots of earnest
debates, mixed with lots of adolescent fun. Kate was in a world a
million miles from that which she had experienced at home. She took
to it, knowing herself for the first time.

Tonight that self-certain, middle-aged Kate surveyed the dinner
table. Echoes from her own past came as Stephen peered over her
shoulder and asked,

"Haven't we got a set of matching glasses?" Kate quashed the
implicit criticism by reminding him of the tray he had dropped last
Christmas.

It was important to Stephen that tonight went well. A visiting
colleague from head office was coming with his wife. He had only
met the man in passing, but knew of his high reputation and influence
in the firm. It was important to maintain his own reputation with such
a man.

It is truly amazing how many words and how much curiosity can
accompany a starter.

"Where did you manage to get such wonderful avocados? Ripe to
perfection. And the sauce – is it your own secret recipe? You must
entertain often." On and on, the colleague's wife, Jean, kept the
tentative business of establishing social contact well controlled in the
incessant babble of dialogue about the meal. Kate felt that she had not
only shopped for and cooked the meal but was now walking around it
inspecting its every facet, exploring its depth as if it were a noble
painting rather than a fast-disappearing collection of meats, fruits and
vegetables. Jean was the major observer and commentator, with the
men pausing reflectively to echo some compliment as they briefly
sipped wine between the clearly enjoyed mouthfuls of food. Kate

moved from the apprehensive hostess, accepting the opening moves in such social encounters as inevitable, to boredom and frustration with her guests apparent wealth of angles on the meal.

As Kate disappeared to the kitchen with the debris of one course and to fetch the next course, her sense of momentary reprieve from the gushing Jean was matched by a change to the masculine concerns which had provoked the evening.

"It's going well," Hugh said to Steve, with reference to the new engineering project.

"I like to think so," said Steve, not wanting to risk a commitment to any aspect which Hugh might want to change later.

It was tactics rather than modesty that lead Steve to skirt warily around these early discussions. But he was saved from being more explicit by the rapturous outburst from Jean at the entrance of dessert. By now Kate was quite embarrassed by the extravagant praise and unwarranted scrutiny of every aspect of the meal and while the extrovert Jean with her bubbly enthusiasm was in no way like her mother, she reflected on the various ways in which 'gracing' social occasions might find widely different, but equally superficial expression.

Kate began to see that for Jean, life was made up of commenting on her social landscape and that while this felt shallow to the busy mind of Kate, for Jean it was savouring realities as they flowed in the wake of her husband's business pursuits.

Steve was feeling a mixture of relief that the first two hours had spared him any over-technical discussion with Hugh and an unexpected anxiety that Jean's microscopic attention to the menu might expose some culinary flaw in Kate's less than precise food preparation.

By the time they moved to the lounge for coffee Steve felt like one of the chorus who, having been denied an earlier cue to centre stage, might now be the main character in the second act of the dinner party. He couldn't have been more wrong. Steve found himself enmeshed in round two of Jean's saga. It changed from food to social encounters on their world travels. It was a change that was natural, if not subtly seamless.

"I much prefer an intimate dinner with friends," she said, "rather than the formal hotel gatherings we've become very used to."

Steve had no doubt that in spite of this being their first meeting she was using the term 'friends' to include this evening with himself and Kate. Kate would have laughed if she had not been busy in the kitchen. 'What a devaluing of friendship,' she would have said, 'it goes with boring theses on 'avocados I have known'.' But then, Kate hadn't heard it and Steve was beginning to warm to Jean's endless but easy chatter which put his own apprehensions for the evening behind him. Stories of dinners in Bangkok and Cape Town, social anecdotes of no consequence and the relaxing wine left Steve feeling good. Only odd encouraging comments were needed to ensure Jean's continued flow. Kate would have mocked Steve's enthusiasm for Jean's reminiscences and said 'you wouldn't have been impressed if they'd have been about Bognor or Sheffield. How could you encourage such a candyfloss brain?'

Kate had been joined in the kitchen by Hugh. He perched on a stool with his wine as she loaded the dish washer and made the coffee.

"You must get weary of having to spend so much time meeting new people and moving on," she said.

"It can be hard," responded Hugh, "but meeting in this sort of way is much more satisfactory than huge impersonal functions. Jean loves it all, with a preference for smaller gatherings. I prefer seeing people in their own situation and getting to know them."

Kate wondered how this was ever possible with such a frothy, garrulous wife. What began to unfold was an intriguing story of Hugh's many solo trips to Third World countries where a simple local meal shared beneath the open sky lead to conversations of life and its struggles and its meaning, undistracted by the affluent trappings of the West. Kate began to see Hugh as a gentle, sensitive man whose own academic and practical brilliance had given him much sycophantic acclaim in the West, but when able to meet with undisguised humanity his own gifts shone. Kate was entranced as he talked about staying with an Indian family and their careful rationing of limited water.

"They each had one small bucketful to last a day. A small amount of carefully measured newly (although hardly fresh) drawn water was used for drinking and cooking purposes, with the small amount which remained used for washing and then reused to sluice out the earth closet. I was given my ration and the discipline of attempting their skill in water management was very humbling. I became very close to that family in their frugal existence and I came very close to myself."

He paused and Kate found no reason to intrude into the silence of his own reflections. It gave her time to picture the poverty of existence about which she would frequently want to talk to Steve, but he dismissed her concern as middle-class do-goodery. 'How can you ever know what's needed in those situations?'

Steve's social concerns were limited to home issues, of which there were plenty, but Kate had a compelling interest in the broader human condition. Steve would tease her about being a graduate in anthropology whose advance studies were the Oxfam newsletter and membership of the local United Nations Association. She was not irritated by his mocking but accepted that their horizons were very different. She often assumed this was the difference between being male and female, as most of the ardent campaigners on Third World issues were women. The same ones she met with and talked with into the small hours at Greenham Common. It was as if her limited suburban existence was only a social limitation; there was nothing that limited her intellectual hunger for, or emotional responsiveness to, the world-wide condition of humankind. Steve regarded it as a hobby which he had to acknowledge was better than flower arranging or cake decorating. But there was a gulf between Steve and Kate. His world was bound by his own specialisation and he was a pragmatist not an idealist – seeing the latter as pretentious and phoney and with none of the hard-headed pressures to 'come up with the goods' as he had to. Kate was hungry for charting new intellectual and emotional territories but knew that Steve would never share her circumnavigations or be interested in hearing about them. Whereas Kate was beginning to sense that Hugh did see the world with eyes like her own. He had said very little, but somehow what he had said struck instantly the familiar chord of searching that was Kate.

"I'll carry the tray," said Hugh as they joined the others for coffee. The fusion of these disparate conversations was left to Jean who, having discovered the coffee was from Kenya, said to Hugh, "Tell them about your trip to Nairobi."

"It would bore them," said Hugh, not so much excusing the telling of his own African experience but wishing to escape the catalogue of high-powered meetings and dinners which Jean was inviting him to share. As an afterthought he said, "I have a couple of photographs in my wallet." He handed one to Steve and the other to Kate. Steve responded with enthusiasm to the picture of the engine which was clearly the object of mutual interest with his own project. He began to ask Hugh all sorts of specific questions about its operation and management. Kate looked at the picture in her hand. The gentle engineer stooped, cradling a black child on one knee and holding the hand of another beaming toddler. His own face shone with the human connection between the little group. Hugh momentarily turned from the dialogue with Steve and said, "Two precious little friends I made," and as he said it his face was renewed with the glow that Kate saw on the picture.

Jean had fallen silent in the busier coffee discussions, but beamed as if her own less substantial contribution had served as a very necessary prelude to the success of their encounter. She kicked off her shoes and said,

"This has been a good evening." Kate warmed to the simple honesty of this woman and glanced again at the human portrait on her lap and said,

"It has."

Soul Search

She sat surrounded by the paraphernalia of domestic evolution and the symbols of familial comfort. The armchair yielded to her body and took her into itself, sporting a shabby cover which bore the marks of the shoe buckles of toddlers, careless coffee-swilling teenagers, snoozing cigarette smokers and the weariness of giving persistent hospitality to the comings and goings of the masculine household. Masculine, that is, apart from Sal, the upholder of the feminine perspective and the perpetuator of myths about the female role. She struggled in her isolation and in the bid to reconcile the opposing pressures to conform and to triumph. Social continuity seemed to have something to do with fulfilling an historical script which gave women their place – one they needed to know and be grateful for – based on having inferior status in the process of perpetuating, nurturing, and servicing the need of mankind. 'Yes, mankind is the right word,' she thought as she looked around a kingdom – yes, another rightfully male word – and saw how the feminine creativity within her was obscured by the male domination of the home. However much she had chosen and arranged (and, it had to be admitted, spasmodically, rather than prescriptively watered) the plants, the landscape seemed much more full of abandoned coffee cups, redundant newspapers turned to the football page, and large grimy trainers. 'This home,' she thought, 'is like a railway station – a very convenient refuge as these men stop in their travels and address their various needs. The fact that the 'waiting room' is tailor-made to meet those needs adds to its attraction; it's all so easy for the traveller, he doesn't have to think about the origins of these services, merely being obliged to make use of them in order not to disappoint their provider!' Yes, this was conformity sure enough and yet for Sal it was only just survival. She felt the claustrophobic pressures which were exhausting and strangling her personal bid for female triumph.

She didn't see this process as one of becoming a latter-day Boudicca or Maggie Thatcher (heaven forbid), but rather as a noble pursuit of herself in which the reality of her femaleness could be celebrated and expressed. She didn't seek the patronizing indulgence of her menfolk, but an aware recognition of the innate humanness of women.

Sal kicked off her slippers, pushed the cat (a large tom) from her knee and put on her shoes. She had been thinking, but even her thoughts felt tricked into a compromised and unreal feminism. It felt like a rebellion, a strike, an energy-sapping bid for something that was eluding her, and she needed to be in touch with herself.

The day was unusually warm for spring in England and people had adopted a suitably instant Mediterranean style of dress – a response borne of some sort of optimistic foolishness or else of a 'striking while the iron is hot' reflex. Whichever it was mattered little to Sal, except that it opened up a wider world; she wasn't forced by an icy wind into the bosom of her male clan, with pop posters and engagement diaries, she could escape to a world bordered by grass and trees. She leapt into the car as if lethargy might remind her of some doubts she had in this enterprise, like the novice swimmer convinced that it's best to stay with her feet anchored in the comforting waters of the shallow end. How amazing to be slipping easily into second gear and moving down the street without an idea of a place to be going. It didn't matter, she would begin to familiarize herself with spontaneity and gauging actions around the instincts of her own desires. Magnet-like she felt drawn to the fresh and burgeoning greenness of the countryside. It modelled a soothing sense of 'being'; not like her armchair but like a primal backcloth of life and growth, against which she could not only find rest but also re-energize her own vibrancy.

She walked a little and came upon a pool set amidst some trees. At first she sat on the grassy bank and then she lay as if permitting a lover access to her prostrate body. She closed her eyes against the brightness of the light and felt the whisper of wind against her cheek, and the earthy dampness reached her nostrils. Sal sensed a light-headedness which came from giving herself both physically and emotionally to the present; her mind took her senses on a guided tour of this rural oasis. A sun-covering cloud induced a shiver which lead Sal into an internal dialogue:–

– 'Who am I?'

'You are Dave's wife, James and Alex's mother, John's daughter, Brian's sister.'

– 'But who else?'

'Who or what else is there, my time is full of them, there is no space.'

– 'Why not, I give them space?'

'Well perhaps that's unfair, there is my teaching job.'

– 'And what opportunity for being myself do I have within that?'

'Not much – the odd project here or there but mostly frenetic chasing, the demands of 'now'.'

– 'So when I've left all my duties who am I then?'

'Nobody – boring, middle-aged and going nowhere.'

Sal stirred, the discomfort of her thinking was matched with the discomfort of lying on the dampening grass. She looked again at the trees; their productivity and the shelter they offered struck her as analogous to the function of her life. They managed to balance the routine of their purpose with a profound dignity of passive vulnerability. She hadn't realized how much pain there was inside until she began this emotional stock-take. From the outside she was a success; people admired the 'nice' sort of family she had managed to grow. True, they weren't the clinically-ordered cornflake ad. family, but reality made them more admirable for that. No one had gone vastly off the rails and she had balanced this with a career. The world projected an expectation of satisfaction, perhaps even self-satisfaction, that allowed for no doubts and no mental scanning of alternatives – heavens, what more could a woman want? A surge of guilt hit Sal as she thought of other families she knew – her friend Isobel, whose husband had left for a younger woman and left her with three rebellious and anti-social children; little Sue Thomas, in her class, whose mother nursed a sick and demanding husband and had had a child killed in a road accident, or all those families in the news – starving, homeless, caught in war. The thoughts acted as a momentary antidote to Sal's personal anguish and she stood up and shook her creased skirt as if to shake away the anguish in her own heart.

'Well,' she thought, 'I'd better get back and prepare supper. I think they all want a meal tonight, but what else they're doing I don't know.' The conformist programme, which was playing in her head, began to filter through more slowly. The ache and emptiness which she had dismissed by giving a global perspective to her own tiny world began to falter. 'I don't change other people's pain and stress by hanging on to my own,' she thought. 'Maybe I would have more energy for all those other worlds if I were not so suffocated in my own.'

Sal walked slowly through the trees. She felt held by their existence, and acknowledged in a way that people, with all the complex range of responses, never communicated to her. Somehow her sense of self was beginning to feel real. She could imagine that poets and artists and composers have the same sense of inner harmony that allows their creativity to capture a spiritual beauty; a beauty others recognise in the objective world of the 'masterpiece', but never feel within themselves. 'Just because I can't translate it into some tangible object doesn't mean the poet's heart is not within me too,' mused Sal as she stooped to hold a primrose in her hand. She was going to pick it but instead just chose to link her own existence with the creamy bloom by touch. Like the butterfly which makes the world its own by lightly sharing a momentary touch. 'I do not need to own the flower, and in owning it hasten its death,' thought Sal. 'It is mine because I touched it and for a minute my senses engaged with its beauty, and for a lifetime, I have the power to bring that to the foreground. A beautiful constellation of nature – its form, its colour, its perfume. I can only be robbed of its beauty by never truly engaging with it or by forgetting it.' These thoughts were deeply warming and helped the embryonic self within Sal to take shape. Time seemed to have no importance and the welcoming springy turf urged Sal on. No thoughts of rushing back came to her, only the desire to feel the present; even this was not a mental decision but a yielding to the feelings which welled up within her.

She looked again at the bright spring sun, an almost forgotten reality in the endless grey of winter, and sensed a physical energy that nature, too must feel when warmth and light begin the process of regeneration. It was easy, and a lightness of spirit caught Sal as she let the heavy thoughts of obligation slip out of her consciousness. She felt the engaged but moving attention of a little child who flits with entranced joy from one delight of sensual experience to another; dashing, not in scant or superficial ways, but thrilling at the vast array of natural things that tempt the eye or ear or touch. The shafts of sunlight showered a striped magnificence through the trees; light and darkness, greenness of every hue, textures rough and smooth, the final death of last year's growth mingled with the new shoots of this year. Nature's tangled untidiness looked like a carefully ordered habitation of life, to Sal. She was not merely a spectator in an alien world but a participant in creation. Her mind could not quite understand the threads of that, but her emotions could; this sense of nature's integrity was more powerful than any neat and rational scientific formula. Sal knew, and although her mind posed hazy questions to challenge the internal process that was taking place, she could ignore them, and needed not the security of intellectual justification. She was beginning to feel an inner liberation that was not achieved by debating oneself out of an oppression or beating the oppressor into confessed retreat, but rather a wholesome connection with herself.

Sal reached a gate that was the boundary between the wood and fields beyond. She leaned on the gate, absorbing what met her eye and what was happening to her feelings. It seemed that the meeting of this human being with the world was a true celebration of life. It was special and thrilling and new and energising and held both the moment and eternity, all in the same span. Sal experienced it like that moment when she was expecting James, and she first felt him move within her own body. It was a mystery, an experience, but beyond and not needing comprehension. A grandeur that was powerful (she seemed to hold the entire world within herself) and humbling (she was the agent but not the true creator of this spark of life). To capture and recapture this gave Sal a sense of excitement followed by fear. Fear that transient ecstasy is rendered unreal because it is passing. But no, her mind took over to heal her anxious feelings – 'Is a rose less beautiful in its blooming, because one day it will die? Is cradling a baby not to be treasured because the baby becomes a man? Is the sweet and tender passion of a lover no more than yesterday's garbage because it is anchored by time and space?' These questions chased through Sal's head and to each she vocalised to the world,

"No... no... no." She was startled by the rising volume of her own vehemence. As she climbed the gate she smiled and let the discovery which came from this internal dialogue rush and settle in her brain and heart. In the field the grass was growing on the rutted furrows of last year's harvesting; easy, like the steady tide rising and falling in earth made ready for crops. Nature seems not to be easily put off by human intervention but quietly continues to be true to itself, barely deflected from its most natural expression. Sal needed to walk carefully so as not to wrench her ankle or trip on the uneven ground.

Sal looked at her watch – she did it a hundred times each day, sometimes to check how much more of the interminable 'double period' still had to be endured; at others it was a kind of reflex punctuation of a life determined by time. In the same reflex way she exclaimed,

"It can't be, I should have been home more than an hour ago." At the same time she missed her footing and fell headlong. She let out a cry as her leg caught the hard hummocky ground; the suddenness of the fall, the sharp pain in her leg, and her startled lungs unable to catch the breath she missed as she hit the ground, dazed her for a moment. She lay on the uncomfortable ground re-orientating herself. The sun, still warm, was creeping lower in the sky, and she felt the sudden loneliness of being in a strange place and needing physical help. She roused her resourcefulness, realising that the damage was minimal, and that she could make her return to the car providing she went slowly and selected an even path. She limped forward with the tunnel vision of one who must avoid further hazards, and with the sensory limitation of one who is only able to register physical discomfort. She wished so much that she was with Dave or one of the boys, and not alone. This careless tumble would have engaged their attention and sympathy at least until she reached home. The liberated woman by the gate suddenly sprang to rebuke the self-pitying Sal. 'Oh, so you can only manage on your own if all is going smoothly?' She smiled at the unintended irony of this last word, given the uneven earth that had tripped her.

Having walked, she guessed, about half the way back to the car, although she was not entirely sure that she was on the right path, Sal felt very sick. She sat on an uprooted tree and felt the wooded world spin around her. Suddenly a voice announced the presence of another human – a woman, one of those who stay the same for decades, giving no clue as to age but having a sensible, neutral appearance.

"Can I help? I saw you sit down rather suddenly and wondered if you were not well."

"I tripped a while ago," Sal said, "and I felt rather faint." The woman took a thermos from her minute back pack, which looked like it would hold nothing, but contained everything. Sal quietly sipped the tea. Neither woman spoke – there was an easy silence between them. As the world steadied before her eyes Sal looked at the woman and thanked her. She was struck by the self-contained strength of the woman, whose steady eyes warmly acknowledged the thanks.

"Now how can I help you?" she said. "Is your car near here or are your family waiting for you somewhere?"

"My car is parked in the lay-by at the start of the wood and my family will be waiting at home, wondering where I've got to."

"Oh," said the woman, "my question was not about the expectations of family so much as whether you were meeting up with them on your walk. It's amazing isn't it how our responsibilities stretch endlessly even into the secluded byways of our own space." Sal laughed. 'This woman's observations are on target,' she thought.

"I often used to walk this way," said the woman, "when I needed to disengage from life's stresses and reconnect with myself. That was when I was teaching, and nursing my mother."

The woman told her story with a matter-of-fact, un-self-pitying directness that was refreshing to Sal. She was clearly someone who had balanced responsibilities without being robbed of herself. She was unemotional, unlike the demanding way that so many people are when they catalogue what life has brought, but she was full of the warmth and gentleness which had sheltered her humanity from the destruction of painful experience. Sal had no desire to stop the woman's quiet monologue or find rejoinders from her own experience, but just to listen and feel soothed in the presence of another. She knew too that when the woman fell silent and returned her gaze to Sal, it was with the eyes and ears of one who listens, not just as an act of not speaking, but as a lovely gift to the other, a gift that aids liberation and self-knowledge. As one who is deft with a jigsaw she quickly pieced together Sal's tiny disclosures, and saw the wider vista of confusion and hurt.

"You may be interested in this," she said, unfastening the back pack again. "I brought it to read when I stopped for a bite to eat. I always read the job page in the education section in *The Guardian*. My teaching days are long since over and I was never free to move around but my weekly muse on 'what might have been' serves as a gymnasium for my imagination, rather like reading exotic travel brochures. I enter new situations in my head. I make mental choices and consider options that are not real – no, not possible – but very real. In other circumstances I would have followed my desires and instincts into crazily different routes, not the one that life presented to me. I sometimes think of myself as a prisoner or hostage, perhaps over-dramatically, totally at the mercy at what malevolent circumstance hands out, but kept sane by the infinite universe of freedom in my mind and heart. Yes, we teachers sometimes neglect the heart, subduing in our pupils and ourselves anything that deflects from the programmed output of rational – that's a laugh – thinking. The more we subdue our feelings the more out minds are subverted into irrational thinking and behaviour. I've talked too long and it's getting cold. I'll walk with you to the car."

The woman took Sal's arm, not as an act of power by the carer over the needs of another, or as a self-conscious act of righteousness, but as a straightforward human gesture. Sal experienced it in this way and felt the care of this woman did not rob her of her own autonomy. They spoke their farewells and thanks at the car with no need to linger or pluck from this encounter more than the simple experience it had been. Rather like the primrose, Sal could feel united with the woman without wanting to take the heart from her kindness.

The throb in her leg was less and she drove steadily and with caution until she reached home.

"Where have you been? We were worried," said Dave, checking the progress of a frozen meat pie in the oven.

"Bye, Mum, can't stop, I'm out tonight," said James, devouring an ungainly sandwich and slipping into his jacket.

Sal gave minimal information about her absence except to give details of the fall. Some attention was diverted to her leg, with the anxiety of those who might be inconvenienced by an out-of-action wife and mother. Dave made some tea and, although it was hot and fresher than that in the thermos, it lacked the accompanying gestures of human connection which the woman had made. Sal glimpsed a grief within for all the lost humanity in this over-peopled world. Her menfolk settled back into their routines, able to function when Sal was in her place. She idly took the paper, given by the woman, and read the columns of job vacancies. Six months' teacher exchange to Canada – what a thought! She let her mind drift over it like a mother caressing her new child. Why not – she could think about it couldn't she? As the woman had said, there is liberation in one's head as well as in actions, but it doesn't have to stay there.

"I've been thinking Dave, what would you say if I applied for a teaching exchange to Canada?" She chose an inopportune moment; Dave and Alex were captivated by the closing minutes of a one day county cricket match.

"Sounds good," said Dave absent-mindedly. "Oh, by the way, your father rang. Can you slip over sometime and help him with his curtains? He's spring cleaning. Isn't it wonderful how he copes?"

Sal fell with a heavy heart into this male world and reflected upon what choosing might mean for a liberated woman.

Waiting

Margaret sat still and neatly in the waiting room. No one knew she was here except Father O'Sullivan. She had been his housekeeper for thirty years and had asked for some time off to attend the hospital. He had looked over his spectacles, from behind his newspaper, silently asking an explanation.

"Women's problems," said Margaret.

Strange how men cause more problems for women than their reproductive systems, but in common parlance it allowed for the closing of a private door, which was what Margaret wanted and it was instantly achieved.

"Is there food for the cat?" asked Father O'Sullivan, not looking away from his muesli and *The Independent*. "I'll put something out for him if you're late back," he responded to her affirmative reply.

The source of her medical difficulties were not only unmentionable in the presbytery, but aroused no discussion or expression of concern. Margaret felt neither disappointment nor irritation that this should be so. Her role as virgin tender of the parish priest was as symbolic of her unshared thoughts and feelings as it was of her unshared body.

Her family had been saddened by her refusal to follow their wishes and join the convent as a nun, but for Margaret even that celibate community of women would have wanted from her a level of personal giving that would breach the wall of her introversion. She redeemed her situation somewhat by successfully applying for the post of housekeeper to the priest at the Church of the Assumption.

"There is no greater work for God than to be servant of his servant," said her mother.

Margaret thankfully sank into the oblivion afforded by a satisfied enough family, a quiet priest given to seeing her as a servant and the obscurity of an acknowledged but almost invisible role in the community.

Invisibility was a condition that was most comfortable for Margaret. As the third of six children her order in the family didn't demand much attention, and the role of 'little mother' to her youngest brother gave the approval she sought. She learned early that life is easiest if you don't draw attention to yourself. The odd scuffle with Sister Pauline at the convent school was confirmation enough that whispering a joke to your neighbour during RE isn't worth the mirth and friendship that might go with it. You might say that Margaret lived her life as if she were holding her breath – not daring to fill her lungs for fear the air might be poisonous. Routines filled her life, not longings or imaginings. Marriages in the family only brought to consciousness what was not for her. Not that anyone had said she was not the marrying kind; she was pretty, indeed with a little more daring in her dress – twin sets were rather outdated – she could have been attractive. She was intelligent, but few people would see it, least of all Margaret because the predictability of her living and conversations never uncovered her potential.

Now she was in a situation that afforded no precedent, no guidelines to steer her unobtrusively.

"Been waiting long?" the restless young man suddenly inquired. Margaret looked up, and a ready smile opened the passivity of her face.

"Quite a while," she said, and without the editing process that might have left it there added, "waiting for some test results."

"Me too," said the young man, "or rather, my wife," He laughed awkwardly as he looked at the 'gynae' clinic notice. Margaret smiled back.

"They don't realise how worrying waiting is," said Margaret.

It was a gesture of empathy with the young man's restlessness rather than a statement of her own discomfort. She had hardly allowed a conscious recognition of anxiety within herself, not out of any martyred constraint but from years of holding her emotions in anæsthetized distance from awareness.

"Serious, is it?" inquired the young man, in turn seeing Margaret's statement as a self-disclosure, more than interest in him.

"Could be," said Margaret with a smile that held the true pain at bay, anxiety masquerading within the understatement.

"Cancer?" inquired the young man.

His directness was not so much an indelicate intrusion but a refreshingly open way of communicating. The genuineness that lay behind the question touched a spot in Margaret's current vulnerability that produced an equally open response, surprising to her and easily accepted by the young man.

"It may be cancer of the womb." She had no problem with this word – womb – when part of the liturgy or in Christmas carols, but suddenly identifying such a personal part of herself to someone she didn't know, and a man at that, caused her to blush.

"It's amazing what they can do," said the young man, thinking her discomfort was about the disease, not its site. "Take us," he said, "we've been trying for a baby for seven years. I always wanted children. Bev wasn't so keen until she thought we couldn't have any, then she became really broody. We saw the doctor who gave us various bits of advice about the best time to conceive and so on. We tried and tried but nothing happened so now they are trying this test-tube baby method. Today we should know whether she's pregnant or not."

Margaret listened to the young man's account of cooperation with nature and science and realised how much more comfortable she was with the idea of immaculate conception rather than with the writhing antics of sex. The young man had made it sound all very clinical and everyday but she hardly dared let her thoughts roam around the intimate exchanges of physical love. Just the sterile gloved hand of the surgeon exploring her virginity had felt both physically and psychologically disturbing. Had this medical entrée into the holy of holies technically robbed her of her virginity? It seemed one of the few noble characteristics of human control worth guarding and feeling pride in. Margaret was not in the habit of letting her mind wander into the torrid waters of sexuality, but somehow her own condition and the frank disclosure of the young man had opened a door onto thoughts and feelings she liked best to ignore. A phrase from the prayer book came to her mind, 'the fruit of her womb', and Margaret suddenly saw this young man and his wife excitedly hoping for the fruit of new life in her womb while for her the fruit of her own womb could be death.

A passing group of nurses diverted their attention and a silence fell between them. The nurses, young and slim and full of their own immediate concerns, chatted light-heartedly and jovially, not registering that the place of their everyday work was full of heavy and anxious foreboding for many of the people they served. For Margaret and the young man their life course could be changed, and the noisy flippancy of the nurses felt like some insensitive music-hall intrusion into the tender place of experience. It was a passing similarity to the rest of life – the unhappy juxtaposition of grief with the whimsically ephemeral; a meeting point that hurts and isolates.

A door opened.

"Mr Noble, would you like to come this way?"

"This is it," said the young man to Margaret.

"Good luck," she whispered.

Margaret sat alone in the clinic amongst rows of chairs, made sadly casual by the remnants of earlier patients – old magazines, coffee cups, redundant appointment cards. The reception desk was piled high with record files, some crisply new, others bulging and worn, like the people who carried a history of pain and suffering. There was a silence and power in the air which was dehumanising, and Margaret somehow felt that the most serious thing which could befall human kind was lost and minimised by the 'system'. What did it matter to anyone here that she might be dying? All this came to Margaret more as a feeling than a thought and it registered as an emptiness in the pit of her stomach.

"Miss O'Riley, please," shouted a nurse from half a dozen cubicles down the corridor. Margaret got up, shaking inside, but slow and steady on the outside.

'This is it,' she said to herself, echoing the words of the young man.

Margaret entered the waiting room to see the young man and presumably Bev sitting stunned but clearly elated.

"Good news?" Margaret asked.

"Yes, we've made it this time," said the young man. His glazed but happy demeanour switched suddenly to a clear focus on Margaret. "And you?" he said.

"Not good," she said in a whispered and cracked voice that squeezed its way through quivering lips. He put his arm round her shoulder. It was a quick gesture, but one of real human warmth, when words serve no purpose. It wasn't patronising or dismissive but a human connection which Margaret had rarely experienced. She knew that for all the joy and hope in the life of this young man he had for a moment entered her world of fear.

"We'll take you for a cup of tea," he said, "and then can we take you home?"

"The cup of tea would be lovely," said Margaret, "but I only live ten minutes walk away and I'll be glad of the fresh air."

"Okay," he said and the trio moved towards the almost empty WRVS canteen.

"Your husband told me about your hopes for a baby," said Margaret to Bev, "I'm really pleased for you." Bev smiled, knowing that now was not the place to spill the wonders of her pregnant state, but also knowing that Margaret was entering, if only for a moment, her world of joy from her own of – she knew not what. They sat quietly over the mugs of hot, strong, sweet tea. Although their thoughts were individual there was a communication between them that happens at times of joy and pain.

Margaret got up.

"I'll be going now but thank you for the tea. I hope all goes well."

"Thank you," said the young man and squeezed her hand. She knew he didn't know what to say but she took it with her as a token of caring for what might lie ahead.

Reflections

It wasn't a noisy or violent end, just sad and inevitable. Tony and Pam had drifted apart, finding fulfilment with people and activities that could no longer be shared. It was difficult to know when the separating began. It was as imperceptible as natural growth – tiny and hardly visible and then full-grown and distinct with no one seeming to notice the process in between. Pam wondered whether it was more sad because they had lost the sensitivity to recognise the movement apart. Would it have been better for a violent eruption to fracture the bond between them?

Pam sat on the bench, absentmindedly looking across the river. It was still, with just an odd whisper of a summer breeze occasionally whipping tiny ripples on the surface of the water. The ducks chased and chattered and then subsided into isolated cruising amongst the reeds. Pam's attention was suddenly caught by two swans, proud and majestic, patrolling the river bank. The still water reflected two shadowy partners, their movements synchronised. There was a haughty majesty in the black eyes that swivelled to view with disdain the world of which it expected notice and approval. The silent harmony of the two birds needed no sophisticated choreographer, their instinct took the duo into matching glides and turns. Pam thought of the early days with Tony. They too had known a harmony that came from instinct rather than negotiation. She wondered if the sense of well-being that comes from such togetherness is felt by swans as well as people. The thought reminded her of her single state and she got up from the bench as if to rearrange the molecules and disguise her aloneness. She wandered close to the river bank where a young woman was looking hot and flushed with the insistent demands of her daughter for something to feeds the ducks. The reality of an exhausted picnic bag failed to quell the child's persistent wail. Pam pulled out the rather squashed cheese roll which she had not finished and gave it to the child. The beam was far more rewarding than the nutritional benefits that would have come from eating it. Pam stooped down with the little girl to help her make the most of throwing tiny morsels to the ducks. As she leant forward she could see her own reflection in the still water, while that of the child was just an outline of blond hair, the features hidden in the ripple of a fishy air bubble. 'This was how it used to be when Claire was little,' she thought. The memory floated first through her feelings – a mix of cosy happiness and grievous loss – and then forced itself into her head with all the snapshot memories reminding her of the early years as Claire's mother.

"Ducks like bread," smiled the little girl in response to Pam's outstretched palm of crumbs. This tiny human being was totally engrossed with 'the now', the anguish and temper of five minutes ago was quite forgotten and the future of no interest. Her whole being was alight with the unfettered and complete engagement with the river bank and the ducks and the bread and her own part in orchestrating feeding time. For a second Pam identified with her. She looked down and smiled at the child and felt the warm sun on her face and arms, the soporific lapping of water on the river bank, and the comical antics of the birds. But somewhere in growing up, sophistication and responsibility had pulled her into a world of schedules and relationships, and, like the relationship with Tony, perspectives are lost and it's impossible to put a time or a place or a reason on their loss – they're just not there any more.

Pam's smile changed from the sunny spontaneity of enjoying the present, to the cynical smirk of one who is hurting too much to be held by the present.

"Say 'thank you' to the lady," the girl's mother said.

"Thank you," echoed the child, hardly paying attention to what had been asked of her. The ducks were still too interesting.

"That's all right," said Pam. She stood up and ambled along the foot-worn path that bordered the river.

There was a whole weekend ahead and Pam had no plans except that she had booked in at The Royal. She wasn't even sure why she had done it and increasingly thought it might not be a very good idea. It was something she had done on the spur of the moment. Like she and Tony had done so many times in the past. Well, perhaps it wasn't that they'd been to this place so many times in the past, it just seemed like that when she reflected on significant markers in their relationship. They first stayed there when they were students at Oxford; Tony had acquired a car and he had said that he knew of a nice little pub on the river that did Sunday lunch. He was obviously proud and invigorated, not only on account of the car, but having a girlfriend too seemed the magical combination of ego-raising factors for a young man of twenty. Some months after that they had spent the night there. They had had the furtive anxiety of people struggling with conventions which they couldn't comfortably disown, but they managed. The excitement of being in love distracted them from likely parental or moral disapproval and indeed the whole world seemed distanced by the all-pervading wonder of being physically and emotionally bonded to another human being.

There were numerous afternoons sprawled on the grass unravelling philosophical arguments, or spent in the repetitively delighted dialogue of lovers. They stayed for one night, the weekend before their graduation. It felt like a ritual to mark the end of their student days – they reminisced and made plans.

It was years later when Claire had had a longish spell of bad nights and Pam's mother offered to stay for the weekend to give Pam and Tony a break.

"Where shall we go?" said Pam, quite sunk into a world bordered by the High Street, the Welfare Clinic and the house.

"Let's go to The Royal," said Tony. They giggled, stepping almost instantly into a setting of indulgence and freedom from responsibility. It had been wonderfully restful, although Tony had felt that the time had somehow been wasted as Pam seemed to sleep all the time. There had been no students around, but just a few very middle-aged couples having a very middle-aged mini-break. It was different outfits for each meal; designer sports gear at breakfast (meant for idling and posing in, certainly not for sport); casual but smart for lunch and decidedly chic (or common, thought Pam) for dinner. She enjoyed people-watching, but she did it not so much with the critical eye of the student but with the eye of an exhausted mother envying and yet despising the freedom of the moderately well-heeled, middle-aged middle-Englander.

The flavour of that weekend had broken the spell of The Royal. Or maybe the reality of their love was more fragile. It had been a welcome weekend, but Pam had wished they hadn't been. She shared her ambivalence with Tony, who laughed and spoke as one for whom those early days at The Royal were fiction rather than real. Whichever it was, the fact that time had faded their romantic sharpness mattered little to him. For Pam it was very painful.

When Claire was about ten Tony had a business trip to the States. Claire missed her father enormously and Pam didn't know how to deal with this new dimension of family experience.

"I'll take you to The Royal at the weekend and show you our old haunts." Claire was enthusiastic, not least because a curtain was opening on her parents and their past, which was also a measure of her own growing up. The days were a success; Claire welcomed the proximity to her mother which was deepened by the dreamy recall of something which she recognised as special without knowing or needing to know what it was. For Pam it hardly mattered that Claire was there, she was lost in the magic of her own story, and strangely Claire did not feel excluded; she enjoyed vicariously the vague something, dreamy and exciting.

That must have been fifteen years ago. Pam and Tony had called once or twice for lunch when they had been travelling that way, but the idea to stop for a meal was more about being familiar with its location and not having to think of an alternative, rather than rushing to thrill the memories with reminders of special times. These functional retreats to The Royal tarnished its place in Pam's mind. It had become ordinary, or perhaps that is all it had ever been. But even then there was an unreflected philosophical assumption that growing away from one's youth is a process of leaving spontaneity and love and excitement behind. Life provides many other sober responsibilities and, if you're lucky, interesting, if busy, schedules.

So there she was dipping into her store of memories and feelings; experiences that had been recorded and stowed away for years. Pam lay on the bed, tired with the feelings that had rushed to embellish the memories. She booked an early evening meal, relishing the thought of an early night and a book. She roused herself to dress for dinner and was curiously self-conscious about the 'look' she wanted to achieve. It was odd, she was used to eating alone when dashing between meetings or deciding not to cook for herself in the evening, but somehow The Royal was different. She had only previously experienced it as one of two and in the early days, as half of one. Now she wanted to look not like a deserted woman dining alone or as a hardened business woman functioning autonomously, but as herself, neither drawing concern nor unwanted interest from anyone else in the hotel. She had brought more clothes than she needed and tried several combinations before settling for a plain yellow linen dress. She brushed her hair and sat in front of the mirror. The dim light from the bedside table hardly did more than allow an outline view of her face – quite unlike the fluorescent strip above her own built-in dressing table. For a moment she saw the student, shimmering with love and anticipation and anxiety as she attended to the body which had just been so delightfully loved by Tony. The lines of laughter and pain were smoothed in the shadows to the soft bloom of youthful skin. What had happened? 'This is the same person – inside still the same – or is it?' Was there a scar of pain in the heart even more disfiguring than the tighter, drier skin on the face and throat of this middle-aged woman? She looked away, the pain reached her eyes which stung with brimming, unshed, scalding tears. She tied her long hair back in a black velvet ribbon – loose was for more blatant social occasions, a French pleat for work, this seemed a reasonable compromise.

She felt nervous as she walked down stairs. 'This is foolish,' she thought, but her confidence was suddenly under attack from all those images from the past. She neither wanted this pounding introversion or the energy required to speculate about the lives and loves of her eating companions – a favourite pastime for Pam and Tony when they were younger. It was as if the fanciful stories and the playful ridicule made the world an alien place that could not cross the moat to their sane and deliciously self-contained contentment. Apart from the energy it needed, it lost the fun if you couldn't speak it out and each add another line, another element to the crazy story.

"Would you like a drink first, madam, or to go straight to the dining-room?"

"I'll go straight to the dining-room, thank you."

"This way, madam."

Pam felt as if she might do something foolish like trip over or knock something off the table as she walked by the elaborately prepared boards of feasting. With relief she reached a table, more prominent than she would have liked, but obscure enough, she guessed. Having chosen and ordered her meal she sat, unsure about where to focus her attention. Suddenly her eye was caught by a reflection of herself. At the end of the room was a mirrored wall made up of squared sections. She looked quite elegant, she thought, and smiled at her vanity, seeking to make the most of anything which might divert from her aloneness, much as a prisoner must invent mental games to play in the restricted environment of his cell. She chose to analyse the view by looking section by section at the content of the mirrored squares. Parts of faces and bodies, leafy outcrops from large plants, segments of tureens and food receptacles from grander banquets. It was like a jigsaw in reverse. Taking apart the whole and dissecting it into component shapes, mysterious in their incompleteness. She remembered going to art class once and being taught how to compose a picture by drawing a grid and paying attention to each part in turn and ending up with something complete. The game ended with the arrival of soup but was resumed as she waited for the main course. This time the focus was more specific, it was upon herself. Unlike the illusion created by the shadow in the bedroom, here was an illusion created by distance. Perhaps she could play the speculation game as if she were the voyeur and not the subject. 'I wonder why that charming woman is eating alone?' she thought. 'Perhaps she's having much needed space away from the demands of a husband and a lover. She is enjoying being herself without need to console or cajole the fractious needs of her partner.' As her crazy, imaginative musing preoccupied her she suddenly realised the charming woman was looking very relaxed. One mirror square showed a peaceful easy face, another a gently supportive hand beneath her chin, another the well brushed hair framing her neck and yet another the plain gold necklace given long ago, prettily gracing her throat. Eating became functional and the taste of lamb and rosemary became a backdrop to a greater sense of well being. Her body was at peace and for the first time since she left London she felt the self-conscious thrill of being herself.

Pam rested well and long and awoke to the penetrating shafts of sunlight illuminating a dancing line of dusty air. She stretched and felt the wonder of her own body stirring with easy wakefulness. She had brought a bundle of letters and she knew that the task she had set herself was to read them. Was it masochism, or grief, or anger that set this task so firmly on the weekend agenda? Some of the letters were fragile with the frequent folding, but it was many years since they had been read with that kind of eagerness.

Pam began by putting them in order. Either they had a date or she knew by looking at them which part of the relationship with Tony had been punctuated with which message. She felt exhausted by confronting this visible part of the past and returned them to the folder. She would read them later.

The easiness of her physical waking contrasted with the disquiet of her emotions. Yesterday had been fine and she felt as if she had achieved a new skill, much as you must feel when you've come through the challenge of an outward bound course – exhausted but satisfied. But why the shadow of anxiety? Of course she might bundle the letters away for the time being, but the task remained, and her feelings could not so easily disengage from the mission of the weekend as her decision to avert her eyes from the messages on the paper. 'This is ridiculous,' she thought, 'I must just get on with it.' She sent for a pot of coffee, slipped into a dressing gown and sat by the window. The morning had a steady brightness which promised to hold out for the whole day.

Pam began to assemble the little bundles in chronological order – the early notes, casual but eager, anxious to save face in the event of their sentiments being unreciprocated, but holding cryptic messages of love for the discerning recipient. They were easily recognisable, pages from student notepads but embellished with flowers, or suns or patterns. Then came the more overtly passionate. The tender sharing of love which engendered words of unambiguous and complete devotion written on cards or notelets with pictures that were a reflection of the sentiments contained within them. And then the formal hotel paper sent from business trips; at first the conscious flaunting of a lifestyle in the ascendant, brash and funny to Pam and Tony, and then the familiar and functional way of communicating on business trips. All these had been punctuated with birthday and anniversary cards originally chosen for their aptness and completed with a personal note and more lately chosen with commercial neutrality and containing nothing but a brief signature. To these Pam had added two recent letters, not from Tony but written on his behalf from his solicitor; formal documents of intent with reference to property.

Even categorising them confronted Pam with the pattern of her life with Tony. Cold with emotion, she sipped her coffee and began to read them:–

62

'Steve is having a party on Sat. Would you like to join the gang? His rooms are splendid and he has a wonderful sofa whose shape and cover I'd like to introduce you to! I know how you like arty things. See you soon.

Tony.'

'Mr Tony Groves has asked me to inform you that he has made arrangements to collect those selected items of the matrimonial home which you have mutually agreed should now become his property on — The antique sofa which earlier he had indicated might remain in your possession, he now claims on the basis of its having been part of his family inheritance. Should you wish to contest this change from the earlier agreement, I would ask you to indicate your intentions as soon as possible.

etc. etc.'

'How odd the way the material world impinges on our story,' thought Pam. That musty old student sofa which must have felt the raucous and beery bodies of its temporary owners and heaved to their clumsy sexual endeavours as they served their apprenticeship as 'men', and then this grander piece that graced their home in which, had they lived in greater splendour, Tony would have cordoned it off with ropes, National Trust style, to protect against a wayward shoe buckle, a crumb, a sticky finger, and hence the disapproving gaze of his long-dead mother. Pam was much too practical to feel anxiety about such things but she had grown to love the sofa and its lovely welcome in the hall as she opened the front door. 'You funny old thing, always there with your arms outstretched, but nobody comes to be embraced,' or, 'You're like an old duchess – grand, but not a scrap of use.' It was these passing conversations with the sofa as she came and went over the years that became a joke. Tony used to tease her about the maidservant waiting in the hall for her return, or the family pet patiently keeping guard by the door. The sofa personae changed, but it was always a person and not a thing. It was the final straw, though quite within his rights, that Tony should now take it. What has a sofa to do with love anyway? 'Nothing,' thought Pam, but just the same there was something. As our bodies are contact points with the world so things become reference points, of significance beyond their material worth.

Pam struggled in her head with the meaning of her relationship with Tony; did it never have any significance because it did not in the present? Was the test of its validity measured by eternity or was it enough that it was once? Does indifference now, negate love then? Was it all an illusion? Is the pain part of losing or waking up to pretence? She always felt that if love wasn't forever then it wasn't real and yet, as she sojourned painfully through the papers, a smile of recognition would curl her lips, a phrase make her feel as if she'd missed a breath and through a time warp been returned to the immediacy of some emotional reality that was part of the present. Footsteps outside the door made Pam glance up and, in so doing, she made immediate eye contact with herself in the mirror. The shadows were gathered on her brow, and pain in her eyes reminded her that a still youthful and energetic mind does not reverse the toll of passing years. This image and the papers were too much, the tears began to flow, first gently and then punctuated by heavy sobs, a deluge of liquid pain streaming down her cheeks. The contemporary Tony would have chided her self-pity and the sentimentality of her reflections. She guessed that he would have been embarrassed and then dismissive of his own youthful history; seeing it as a rather insipid part of the journey to maturity. Was it Tony who had become hard or Pam soft? Such a simplistic and yet important question was only answered in Pam's head by the undeniable truth that their love had died. The word 'death' seemed such an apt but surprising confrontation with the passing of their relationship, as if after a long terminal illness the dying had been forgotten in the routines of disengagement.

"Death: that's it," she said aloud. "How could I have missed the truth?"

Having been to the florist Pam went to the river bank. She was shaking and yet elated. She walked slowly, her mind turning over the history of her life with Tony. She reached a quiet spot beyond the day-trippers and the anglers. Looking at the two roses in her hand she caught again the togetherness of their love and then, tearless, she threw them into the river.

"Good-bye and, and ..." the words were hard but important, "thank you." She watched as the two blooms, still entwined, bobbed on the water. Slowly entering the flow of the mid stream they became separate and, having kept parallel for a little while, moved further and further apart. She moved away, tired but at peace.

"Pleasant weekend?" inquired the receptionist as Pam paid the bill.

"I'm ready for anything now," replied Pam reflexively.

She wasn't sure as she said it whether it came from bravado or cynicism, courage or grief. But the girl didn't detect meaning. She only heard the words to which the bland and well-rehearsed receptionist-speak response was made.

"Do come again – it's obviously done you good." She was eager to make a commercial opportunity out of an apparently satisfied customer. Pam smiled, not ungraciously, but knowing that the importance of having said goodbye is to move on.

And After the Rain . . .

Thousands of tiny rainbows glistened in the grass as the sun struck each blade. It had been one of those days when the rain had continued in a steady stream, and the unexpected evening sunshine came as quite a surprise to Edgar. He climbed slowly up the hill holding tightly onto the bunch of flowers wrapped in fancy flower-shop paper. Edgar had waited all day for the rain to ease off and now he had been rewarded by this warm spring sunshine, which sank comfortingly on his mackintoshed back. Half way up the hill he paused, not so much out of physical necessity, but to marshal the thoughts that had kept him company since Eadie's death a month ago. He looked down on to the town to see the shafts of sunlight unable to penetrate the black monuments to nineteenth-century wealth; those mills of industry which had given employment to so many in the town and yet had swallowed their souls in return. At least Edgar had escaped that and had managed a position in the bank.

He turned again to make the last few yards into the cemetery. He knew he would have had to come even if the rain had not ceased, and in a way the sun seemed to rebuke his faintheartedness for not making the journey sooner. He had made the same trip each Saturday since the funeral. It was not out of devotion, that had died long since, nor out of a sense of duty, but perhaps because of his training in doing the 'right thing', and long years of nagging from Eadie. 'Trouble is these days people have no respect for the dead. It only seems right that they should visit the resting place regular.' That was typical of her to be so dogmatic about people's social responsibility, even though she had cut herself off from her own family when she had married Edgar. Her folks would not fit in with a banking man like him. They accepted this abandonment knowing only of money coming in a wage packet or from the dole. The world of banking was a closed one to them. Edgar had thought it rather unnecessary for Eadie to be so superior.

After all he only worked on the counter and would certainly never do anything more exacting than issue some travellers' cheques and a small amount of foreign currency to the flighty young typists on their annual pilgrimage to Spain.

His marriage had not so much been a disappointment as confirmation that most of what Edgar had chosen to do had become an anticlimax, almost from the start. He learned to see himself as one of those men who can expect little from life. Perhaps for this reason life with Eadie had been less uncomfortable than it might have been for a man with greater ambitions and ideas for himself.

He recalled the night she came home from work feeling unwell. He'd analysed it as 'attention seeking' but had prepared an evening meal uncomplainingly. The evening had passed quietly. If Edgar was a big disappointment to Eadie at least that night she hadn't said so. In fact, Eadie sitting with her eyes closed while Edgar read the newspaper and his photographic journal (which she kept threatening to cancel because of the increase in explicit pictures) was as near to bliss as he could remember.

Edgar woke next morning and, cheered by the pleasantness of the previous evening, slipped quietly downstairs to make a cup of tea; a treat saved usually for Sundays. He even hummed to himself as he returned with the tray, feeling that his spontaneous act of consideration for Eadie's unspecified malady would certainly bring approval. He set the tray down and began to pour the two cups of tea. Not until it was quite ready did he attempt to arouse Eadie.

At first he had thought it was a trick of hers to escape an acknowledgement of his kindness. Then his pulse rate quickened as he tried to wake her. He stood for a moment like a tailor's dummy, observing the scene but not feeling part of it. Perhaps he should call the doctor, he thought, but it was a few moments before he made a move. Mrs Ellis next door had a phone but he decided he would rather not bother the neighbours. He put on his trousers and jacket over his pyjamas and looked again at his wife. Making sure he had some change in his pocket he walked slowly into the next road to the phone box. He stood staring at the phone as if it was the first time he had been confronted with this instrument of communication. Suddenly his mind became alert and he focused on the mechanics of dialling. Then he stopped, should he ring the doctor or the ambulance? Perhaps the ambulance might be easier, it would save having to apologise for calling outside surgery hours.

On his way back to the house Edgar felt quite incapable of coping with a crisis. The years of succumbing to Eadie's domination had left him quite bereft of initiative. Perhaps he ought to have gone to Mrs Ellis, she was the same organising sort as Eadie, although kinder, he suspected.

He climbed the stairs and found Eadie as he had left her. Sitting on the bed he took her hand in his, an act of tenderness which surprised him but which gave him a fresh confidence in himself. Yes, it was almost pleasant not having to play life's drama with the dialogue written by Eadie, but just to be himself. This spark of the real Edgar began to take hold and it was not extinguished until the doorbell awakened him to the world again. He started almost as if he had been discovered in some improper activity.

The casualty Sister called him into the cubicle where the doctor had just looked at Eadie. It seemed she had suffered a brain haemorrhage and was deeply unconscious. They would call him if there was any further news but perhaps he might like to go home and dress. Edgar had forgotten that he still had his night clothes on, but the border of blue stripes below his trousers and the open necked jacket were in evidence to the Sister.

The tea bar wasn't open so he decided not to linger but to walk home. It was further than he would have chosen to walk, but he became conscious of his appearance and felt that Eadie would feel ashamed if any of the neighbours saw him as they were on their way to work. In compliance with this thought he took a devious route home and met no one whom Eadie knew. He climbed the stairs and looked at the tray on the bedroom floor; a milky film floating on each cup and a brown stain on the spoons were all that was left of his good intention. It was only then as he looked at the cups, the brash floral china one of Eadie's and the plain yellow earthenware one of his own, that he began to think of himself and Eadie. Was she going to die? He had never thought of being the survivor of the marriage. It always seemed that the women lasted longer. In any case she was only forty-nine. The click of the letter-box as the morning post was delivered caused him to start, as though the idea of Eadie dying was in fact his murderous plot. Having shaved and dressed he went to the phone box which he had used earlier. It did not seem nearly so strange now that the street was awake with activity.

He explained the situation to the bank manager, who told him to have as much time off as he needed. Edgar leant on the phone directory. Had he made up the story? His life was just too regulated to absorb this new turn of events.

On returning to the hospital he was sent to the intensive care unit. He sat beside the curtained-off bed, listening to what was going on outside it. It was somehow easier than focusing on the pale face of Eadie.

'I guess if she knew where she was she would be cross she had missed her last hairdresser's appointment,' Edgar said to himself. As Edgar emerged from this unreal world he began to focus on his past life, rather as he understood a drowning man did before his death.

He left the ward to ring Eadie's office (he had forgotten to do it earlier) and to get a cup of tea and some cigarettes. He hadn't smoked for years, Eadie thought it was a dirty habit. She didn't mind people killing themselves with lung disease if they were so stupid, but she was not having ashtrays lying about the place and ash on her furniture. Edgar thought it might calm him and went outside to light up. He found a low wall by the car park and sat on it. The intensive care unit didn't face this way, he thought, and then, as if lighting that spark of himself as well as the cigarette, said aloud,

"And so what, it's up to me."

Simultaneously as he took his first puff a nurse called to him. He jumped from the wall, stubbed the cigarette out and stood to attention in front of the nurse, with the fresh pallor of a discovered schoolboy.

"Sister would like to see you." It seemed a further rebuke for his furtive smoking, and his pale face turned scarlet.

Eadie had already died when he returned to the ward. He took the toilet bag, which he had hurriedly prepared in the morning, and tucked it under his arm. He again set out to walk home. This time because he wanted to think. Think, hadn't he been doing that all morning? He shrugged, they had been daydreams, not thoughts, now he must really think.

The cloud of unreality had still not lifted from his shoulders even as he turned the key in the front door. He looked at the tray still on the bedroom floor and at the unmade bed. He hurriedly tidied the room and went downstairs to wash the two cups and clear away the unused breakfast dishes. He couldn't think while he still might be caught in a state of disarray. Eadie wouldn't like it.

Edgar returned to work after the funeral still in a daze. All the self-conscious and embarrassing words of condolence expressed by his associates passed before him as insignificantly as the rubber stamp he used to complete a transaction at the counter. There were times when he even wondered whether it was his own death he had witnessed. He somehow imagined the other world would feel like being half awake and only partly related to the people around him.

As he stood in the cemetery a passing cloud hid the sun and he shivered momentarily. That feeling of cold jerked him into action and he carefully unwrapped the flowers. There was no headstone yet and he knew it would be a major decision about the inscription, but for the moment Eadie's second-best glass vase managed. He put the dead flowers into the paper and tried to arranged the new ones. He would just seem to have it right when one would swing out of place. He was in no hurry so he continued to battle with the lively blooms.

A voice roused him from his concentration.

"Hi," said the boy as he knelt down beside Edgar. "I've just had the same trouble so I've left 'em. No one's going to know, least of all me Granddad. Me Mam got some cheap daffodils from the market so she sent me up 'ere with these for 'im." At first Edgar was irritated by the interruption but then felt relieved that he could look away from the unruly bunch of flowers.

"Did you have yours from a proper shop? It looks like it with that paper."

Edgar nodded as though having to apologise to the boy for such extravagance.

"Missis is it?"

Edgar nodded again.

"Expect you loved her a lot to buy her flowers like that. Couldn't stand me Granddad. He lived with us and he was always nagging, and wanting me to go errands for 'im. Me Mam's glad he's gone as well, but she doesn't say so. Well grown-ups don't do they? Made me sick at his funeral everybody saying nice things about him. Only days before nobody had a good word for 'im."

Edgar wished the lad would stop, but got up ready to listen him. He was about eight, very scruffy and the sort of boy of whom Eadie

would have said, 'I wouldn't let a child of mine go around like that.'
But then they had never had children. He would have liked them, but
giving birth and dealing with babies had been too primitive for Eadie
to consider. The fact that there had been no 'mistakes' in her plan
gave her an added sense of prestige in her aspiring middle-class eyes.
She was above such basic activity.

It must have been years since Edgar had talked to a child and he
was beginning to like it.

"Why are people so funny? They say all sorts of things they don't
believe and if I say what I think I'm wicked. I only said to me Mam
that I wouldn't bring flowers for that old bugger and she nearly went
berserk. 'Specially when I said if she was so fond of him why didn't
she bring them herself. I didn't say any more 'cause me Dad came at
me with his slipper. Anyway I suppose it's quite nice up 'ere, no one
to nag you and disturb you." The boy laughed at the idea and then
turned to Edgar, "Miss her do yer?"

Edgar nodded again. Well it was true he did miss her, he
confirmed to himself. He reached into his pocket for the cigarettes,
the ones he had bought at the hospital and had never felt able to use
since the nurse had called to him. He lit one and puffed out the smoke
slowly as if, like incense, it carried his thoughts to the sky. Yes, why
shouldn't he if he liked it, Eadie wasn't here any longer so why
should it upset her? He felt, as he had done when he had held her
hand for the last time, a kindling of himself glow within. Perhaps he
might go to the cinema tonight instead of listening to the Saturday
night play as he and Eadie had done for the last he didn't know how
many years. He smiled as he blew out some more smoke. The boy
looked up.

"Me Dad's given up smoking. Says it's bad for yer health, though
he's miserable as sin now. You look as if you enjoy it."

"Yes," said Edgar. It was the first actual word he had said to the
boy, and it gave him a sort of confidence that he hadn't felt for a long
time. 'Nobody has asked me what I like doing in ages,' he thought,
'and here's this little urchin observing the real me.'

"Me Granddad was a real beast, he used to smoke and drink and
swear. I wonder if he's being tormented in hell? I'm sure those
flowers won't do him much good if he is." The boy laughed again.
In this boy's innocent and crude look at death he found his own
feelings take shape. With Eadie he'd only had thoughts and they were

her thoughts. The novelty of actually feeling gave him a sudden sense of being alive and the cloud of unreality began to lift. Perhaps he could book a holiday abroad with the photographic guild and go to their meetings. He smiled at the thought. Maybe he could ask for a transfer to another branch of the bank and find a flat in another district.

With each new idea his spirits lifted. It was not the actual possibilities which charged him but the independence of the ideas. 'Not what Eadie wants but what I want.'

The boy looked up. He had had a go at putting the flowers straight.

"Are they any better?"

"Thanks, but it doesn't really matter," said Edgar, still dreaming of possibilities.

"Well I must be off," said the lad, "I'm off to play football. P'raps I'll see you up here again if I'm sent up with a bunch."

Edgar looked him fully in the face and said, "Perhaps," but under his breath, "I doubt it."

Relative Lives

The phone pulsed its sound into the night quietness and Meg lifted the bedside receiver.

"He's gone," said Trish.

"How's Mum?"

"Sleeping."

"I'll be with you by lunch-time."

The telegraphic conversation belied the communication between the two women, who embraced within the paucity of their words. A lack of emotional articulation joined them in their poignant new grief.

Meg sat on the edge of her bed and reflected. The memories surfaced with a jagged clarity – a jerky sequencing of events and relationships that seemed both distant and present. She looked up and her eyes caught the faded dressing-gown on the bedroom door – her father's gift when she left home. It was his only separate gesture of giving. Usually the choice and the gift were her mother's with 'dad' appended to the tag. She lifted it carefully from the hook. Its smoothness was a mix of its synthetic origin and the wear and tear of many years. The spontaneous smile that came to her lips as she thought back on the history of this ill-chosen, garish gift merged with the tears that were an expression of the connection with the man who had made her and who had just died. The ambivalence of the smiles and tears registered the ache inside, which had begun two weeks ago with the onset of his unexpected illness, but only now erupted into agony. Meg touched the faded brightness of the fifteen-year-old gift and then slipped into it. She shivered as if her body was reacting to this token embrace from her father.

She walked slowly into the kitchen and opened the curtains onto the watery brightness of an early spring day; the dawning sun and clouds changed places in the sky as the breeze chased the threatening blackness first in front and then around the pale ball of light. Meg could not have said how long she watched, but the elements served both as mirror to her own inner senses of blackness and light and as a reminder of some underlying transience of life. Her head could not grapple with thoughts but her heart registered truth.

While the kettle boiled Meg wandered from room to room, her eyes alighting on her domestic trappings as if seeing them for the first time – an awareness that comes with grief. Familiar things seemed strangely unfamiliar, like her grandmother's inlaid sewing-box, part of her visual world since a child. Then it had been part of an impressionistic blur, now she saw it as a crafted object with clear shapes and lines, the creation of a craftsman who had taken pride in its making. It had been chosen and given and enjoyed and now its obscurity and dismissal to the margins of the material world seemed to Meg like a kind of obscenity, in which the talents and loves which had formed and owned it were held of no account.

All of this was taking time. Time she had allowed for any problems on the journey when she had told Trish that she would arrive by lunch-time, not for these half-paralysed, half acutely-conscious reflections. She moved more purposefully to make some toast, but the temperamental electric device which had been a wedding present moved from sluggish underdone to blackened overdone in a matter of seconds. Meg fell to cursing the toaster and instantly thought of her marriage with Jack. How often the toaster had become a catalyst for their early-morning discontent with each other; sometimes it was the cause of personal reprimand, at others the scapegoat for what was too painful to address between them. Jack was dead now – just a few months, and for the first time Meg wondered whether she could regard herself as a widow rather than an ex-wife. Had all of those socially connecting descriptions ceased on the day he left or could she claim some retrospective status that might prompt sympathy, rather than the judgements which went with a failed marriage?

The motorway was busy but, unlike the sharp awareness she had felt earlier for her own flat and its possessions, vehicles and signs, hills and fields passed almost without notice and only as she began to enter the familiar land marks of 'home' did she realise how easy it might be for her own end to follow Jack's and her father's.

"You will have to come back," were her mother's first words. Had she said this over the telephone Meg would still have naïvely thought it was a command connected to the short-term circumstances of death and its aftermath. But Meg knew that her mother was already making long-term plans. For a moment she was closed to the emotional and mental collage which had occupied her heart and mind in the hours since her sister's telephone call. The rich sensations and pictures which had fused the past and present no longer seemed a permitted bitter-sweet reverie of grief but a self-indulgence denied by the demands of her mother. The only passing reverie that came unbidden, as she sought to take control of herself and the situation, was a mental fantasy of her father quietly responding to her mother's words, 'No, Margaret, Meg will do what she needs to.'

This imagined statement of permission from her father to act according to her own conscience and not to the prescriptive demand of her mother swiftly shifted in Meg's awareness to a realization that she could act only in the way demanded of her by her mother. The protective support of her father had now come to an end and without it Meg's own independent resolve evaporated. Meg knew that if she responded to her mother's demands she would be full of resentment, but if she denied them she would be full of guilt.

"There's time to see to that Mum, for the moment we have lots to do," Meg stalled, but it took more energy than she had to be the diplomat and she slipped upstairs to weep daughter's tears alone.

The torture of her conscience drove her to knock at the door of a therapist. It was costly, financially and emotionally, but the crossroads of resentment and guilt had to be faced. The death of her father brought Meg scurrying back to the dilemmas of childhood when her defiance and single-mindedness brought constant conflict between herself and her mother. It was not the major disputes that had etched the scars on Meg's youth but those situations in which her conscience would grudgingly concede that maybe she had been in the wrong.

Meg had always believed that her mother's migraine was a very useful device for getting her own way, but she would never directly challenge her, only circumvent the issue. Such an occasion was the impending school play, when Meg was six. She had only a minor part but her enthusiasm and excitement equalled that of the lead actors. For weeks she talked endlessly of the details of costumes and rehearsals and the mini-world of school life that revolved around Miss James and the play.

On the day of the dress rehearsal Meg's mother was stricken with "one of my heads – I need you to stay at home, Meg. I get very frightened when I get an attack."

Meg had been defiant, "I've got to go to school. It would let Miss James down." The burning in her throat and eyes rose with fierce spontaneity at the very idea of being cheated of the delights of the final crescendo of effort for the play. She knew now what she had not realised then, that she was making Miss James an excuse. It was important not to let her down but it was for herself that she was not prepared to compromise.

Her mother's faint but decisive tone replied, "Meg, I'm not asking you, I'm telling you."

Meg left her mother's room. She felt her heart beat so loud and fast that she thought she might explode with the injustice of the command. There was no way she could be denied the anticipated pleasure of costumes and make-up and the companionship of the project, with all the bonding and confirmation of her place within the social community of Parkfield County Primary.

Meg dressed quickly and said to Trish, two years her junior "You'd better stay with Mum, she isn't well. Tell Mrs Freeman when she calls to pick you up."

Trish began to cry with the unexpected burden of responsibility never previously carried in her four years.

"And don't cry, just tell Mum I had to go."

Meg hurried through the door. The rehearsal was a disaster, Miss James was cross with everyone, including Meg, and the internal anguish was almost intolerable. What if her mother died, what if Trish burned the house down, or ran away or was abducted? The stream of calamities was endless and Meg felt that it was all her fault. Even the kindly placatory gentleness of her father would not be enough to reverse such disasters.

Meg walked home alone. She told her friend Sue to 'get lost' – a phrase which would have mortified her mother but which was said out of self-punishment. What she would most have liked would have been Sue's cheerful companionship to counter the pit of despair.

No comment was ever made at home. Trish had gone to school with Christopher Freeman and his mother, and her mother was lying on the sofa, pale, when she returned. That such profound guilt could be formed and lie encrusted in the psyche for thirty years when so little apparently was said or done to promote it was a mystery to Meg. The telling of this story to her therapist fell and tumbled with the detail of a world drama and with a startling clarity that was profoundly disturbing to Meg.

"But it was nothing," she said. "No one said anything, but I feel it still, the responsibility to the vulnerability of my mother and sister."

The event was revisited many times. With each telling the fabric of the world in which it happened became clear – the pattern on her mother's bedspread, the shoes that Trish wore, Sue's satchel with its missing buckle, the lead player with a cold who sneezed her way through the rehearsal. At times Meg thought the detail came from her imagination but she knew that it was all true. Like an absent resident who rediscovers the qualities and shapes of her house on returning to the home that has been covered in dust-sheets, so Meg was taking off the dust-sheets in the storehouse of her memory.

She hoped that she might be rid of this emotional bondage but, far from liberation, her awakened consciousness roused that original sense of guilt. This guilt must be avenged.

"I've decided to sell up in London and come back to Gloucester," Meg said to Trish.

Suddenly the years of defiant independence which Trish had seen in her sister had evaporated. Trish tried to reason that defiance and independence back, knowing how hard she had fought to break the maternal tentacles which had been lovingly placed but insidiously tightened to hold both women to their mother. Trish had been the one to capitulate. She had never even mentally rehearsed the possibility of her own escape but found a kind of pleasure in fulfilling the limiting and limited vision her mother had for her – the library, a broken engagement ('I'm sure with time you'll see it was for the best.') and domesticity made bearable by the sensitive wisdom of her father.

When she had fully comprehended Meg's intention, Trish said, "I've been thinking too. I've spent many hours talking with Jim about Dad and about me and about life."

This old friend Jim, somewhere between her parents' generation and her own, had been the 'therapist' of Trish's veiled but anguished past. An anguish which she had perceived in a different way from Meg. Conformity had etched its own unconscious pain. She began to feel that spark of her own aspirations catch light and the burden of mediocrity and submission being shed like the butterfly emerging from a redundant chrysalis.

"I'm going to make a new life. I don't know how and I would have done it even if you had not intended to return. In fact I wish you would not renege on your hard-won freedom – but that is for you to decide. I have just realised that the real parental tie was with Father. Now he has gone, I must ignore the phoney trap."

The two women embraced, a loving empathy held the divergence of their past lives and the prospects for the future in a sweet unity. No words were needed to express their understanding of the strange perversity of finding and expressing freedom.

Pure Serendipity

Anna stood looking down the garden from the french windows. Her great-uncle sat in the room behind her, peering studiously at the configuration of pieces left on the chessboard. She no longer had energy for this act of analysis in the closing drama of each game she had played since he had first taught her six or seven years previously. When she was ten she had watched this external passivity combined with mental intensity and seen it as holding something of the mystery of being an adult; a world in which thoughts are not readily betrayed by words or body language; a world not yet understood but glimpsed as holding possibilities for her own potency.

When she was thirteen or fourteen her sense of curiosity regarding the chequered board and its black and white inhabitants changed to frustration. Anna wanted to be part of the process – playing the game and weighing all the possibilities. She pressed Uncle George to share the mental gymnastics with her. So he began to take her thoughts into his pensive world as he spoke aloud the thrills of manoeuvre and counter-manoeuvre. Kings and queens and knights and bishops chasing and dodging to survive the destructive wit of their enemy. Pawns too, finding their own inferiority enhanced by the socially protective role they could afford their mightier kin. The captivating fantasy with all its power struggles too closely echoed the real world of twenty-year-old Anna and she was impatient to leave the game to itself – complete and irreversible.

Uncle George grunted but seemed not to have heard her excuse herself. He was still captivated by the progress of the game, and without need of modern technology he could conjure up an 'action replay' in his mind, for each crucial stage of the journey to checkmate.

Anna walked down the garden. It was a long, narrow ribbon of cultivation that nestled between the other individual creations, which ran from the back window of each house of this Edwardian terrace. Some had been tended carefully and retained their original varied usage, differences defined only by horticultural preference and the skill of the gardener. Uncle George and Aunt Martha's garden was like this. It unfolded from an old brick-paved patio with a sundial, to a pocket-handkerchief lawn surrounded by neat borders. This gave way through a rose-covered arch to a more roughly-grassed area with shrubs and an apple tree and a gazebo nestling secretly between them. On and on the ribbon of land went to a vegetable plot once intensively worked, but now producing only a few salad vegetables. The wilderness and compost heap at the end marked its margin with the world. Before her entrée into the delights of chess this garden had been where her childhood imagination had been deliciously prompted into pictures and encounters of dramatic and romantic kinds which had thrilled her young heart with the endlessness of possibility. That number eleven Winchester Terrace was both like and unlike all its neighbours' gardens added to the fantasy that could be enjoyed within it. Some of the gardens had modern patios with plastic tables, and chairs and lawns strewn with sunbeds and barbecue equipment, some remained the forgotten appendage of busy or careless people, while others hinted at ecological consciences with chickens and organic vegetables. Anna smiled as she viewed this landscape of variety which could not be predicted if one stood at the uniform front doors of these houses.

"Pure serendipity," she mused.

These miscellaneous ruminations connected memories with the present. The chess board and the garden fixed points upon which the infinite variety of experience was staged. Time moved across their surface to ruffle or destroy the players, but their survival or destruction was somehow firmly anchored to pre-ordained patterns of existence. Infinity and finiteness, predictability and surprise were all contained within the symbols of life at number eleven. It was odd to have this consciousness of time and life so sharply focused in her head. It was almost as if the chess game twirled and pirouetted in her mind, matching the dancing philosophical thoughts which were centre stage in her awareness.

As a child, visiting this much-loved great-aunt and great-uncle brought a range and richness of experience, relished by the senses but not analysed by the mind. Dressing up in velvet and satin dresses, fox

furs, and jewelled hatpins, was not a journey into the past but a deep
savouring of the present. Playing 'grown-ups' with cousins Audrey
and Kay was not a rehearsal for the future but was a delicious dipping
into a world of personalities to be understood and ridiculed, now.

Anna smiled as she thought of those excursions to this North
London suburb from her home in Manchester. Uncle George was her
maternal grandmother's brother. He and his wife Martha had no
children and were seen as the 'made good' end of the family. He had
moved to a steady, though unspectacular teaching post in a boys'
grammar school. Their house, from which fields were then visible
(later covered by redbrick boxes for young couples and their two point
four children), was regarded by the Manchester end of the clan as
rural, and so holidays and Aunt Martha became synonymous. Not
that they were frequent, but they were always special and their value
for boasting to one's friends was enormous. Every detail of the house
and garden, the food, the games, the excursions were told with relish
and not a little elaboration. Activities undertaken more than once
entered the oral tradition as ritual and were recalled by, 'Do you
remember when we used to...' No matter the frequency of any such
activity, the enjoyment of retelling was every bit as wonderful as the
experience itself – if not a little better!

Even now as she walked down the garden Anna could feel those
warm summer breezes brushing her arms and legs and the firm,
smooth sensation of bare feet in Clarkes sandals. What kaleidoscopic
memories rose within her! Memories not only recaptured by thought,
but smell and touch – a sensual cornucopia of childhood. And yet this
sudden surge of richness from the past made her look down at herself
– this slim, energetic woman who had just completed her first year at
university.

'Am I now as real as then?' she thought, 'or has entering the adult
world become all analysis, standing back, the observer and not the
participant?' She glanced back towards the house and saw Uncle
George still poring over the chess board. He looked like an allegory
of all that she felt at that moment; a mind brooding on the nature of
life's stage and its events, but losing the subjective delights of being
an actor within it. Her head whirred. Was it merely the inevitable
loss of innocence as she took on the mantle of adulthood or was it a

more insidious invention of a world unable to stay with some of the sharper truths of experience?

Anna had enjoyed her first year at university. She was studying English and her tutor had fired her with a real sense of purpose in her studies. She had hardly dared to admit to herself that A level with Miss Lang had been a bore. It had contained none of the excitement she found with her early-adolescent adventure books. Some of them would hardly have been called literature, but she loved the surprise and intrigue and the limitless images that passed through her mind's eye.

Miss Lang had always insisted that ideas clothed in words, not stories, were at the heart of great literature. It was like being made to explore individual jigsaw pieces without having the pleasure of seeing their combined unity. Anna had protested,

"Why not ideas and stories?"

Miss Lang, with a superior glance above her spectacles, had closed the argument by saying, "When you become a real student of literature you will know I am right." How infuriatingly non-combative! She gave up, settling for what she thought was Miss Lang's limited wisdom, which she hoped would coincide with that of the examiners. The frustration led Anna into an equally intransigent and limiting perspective where she found the predictability of Austen manners and Dickensian morals very trying. She conceded that Shakespeare gave some interesting and significant roles to minor characters and that was a relief. She enjoyed the rhythm and humour of Betjeman and some of the lyrical lines from the Romantic poets, but what she craved was something more. A mystery to be searched out and to give one an entrée into the secrets of the human soul. Yes, that was what Anna was wanting and she was beginning to find it as her tutor led her into the enchanted wood of literature. T S Eliot, especially, touched a tender place in her own yearning. She felt liberated by study which allowed for exploration not limited by a purely didactic perspective.

Her soul, head and heart were being stirred by a strange new alertness. Anna didn't suppose that Uncle George had ever needed to be acquainted with either his heart or his soul. His intellect had served him well enough for his life purposes and the fact that this was tempered by a natural warmth and gentleness was more than adequate demonstration of his humanity. Anna felt sure that if he could

82

uncover the strategy of each game of chess as it lived and died on the chequered board, then no doubt he had a glimpse that was most satisfying to him, of the nature of existence.

"That's not for me," she found herself saying aloud, "not even the clever two-directional movement of the knight or even the mightier power of the queen reflect the infinite variety of the poet's heart or the prophet's wisdom. What happens when these players are outside their chequered domain? Are they really more powerless or do they scoff at the rigidity of their kin?"

Anna was puzzled by the paradox that some rules liberate and others imprison. What of those chessmen, are they more themselves, marching to the limited tune of their own kind, or are they most free when they are removed from the game? If looked at philosophically then perhaps the dismissed pieces become symbols of a freer life, but if viewed practically they become inanimate nonentities removed from the centre of play. 'But life is much more complex than a game of chess,' thought Anna, now able to abandon the limitations of the analogy. She could see that poetry could only really flourish when the creative heart and mind is not confined to issues of survival, and that the wisdom of undistressed reflection can burgeon most powerfully when life is contemplated at several steps' distance.

Anna's mind toyed with these ideas. It suddenly seemed to her that those flashbacks to her own not-too-distant childhood reminded her how much of the mystery is joyfully experienced, but not understood by the child. The adult struggle to comprehend finds both intellectual reason and sensual wonder elusive. This growing insight which linked her past to her present felt to Anna like a warm light at the centre of herself. Having unpacked those layers of history and laid them bare to the scrutiny of her comprehension, she knew with satisfaction that this need not be a process in which the experiential delights of living are sacrificed to mental analysis. Her memories could be stowed away again; complete, bright, undissected. Her head and heart could sing in unison with her soul.

The warmth inside reminded Anna of Rob. She had been feeling confused and desolate since he departed for his European field study. His parting note, casual as always, ended 'love Rob'. What cryptic message lies in that word; a word for lovers reaching the pinnacle of human bliss; a message on myriad Christmas cards sent to reflect all shades of affection – and none; the contrived gesture of warmth between chat show host and celebrity.

'Maybe I don't need to know what it isn't,' thought Anna. 'It is enough to know that for Rob love is no more and no less than the gentle unfolding of tenderness and intimacy with me. That is enough.'

A cloud robbed the rather weak and watery afternoon sun of its warmth. Anna shivered and then walked slowly towards the house. Inside she could hear the gentle tap of the chessmen being placed in their marquetry box. Uncle George handled them with reverence for their power and a regard for their impotence. His reverie had ceased and he would now enter Anna's world of cups of tea and train schedules and news from home.

When Anna stepped into the sitting-room Uncle George was on his knees on the floor. She rushed to help him, fearing his stiff limbs had let him down.

"I seem to have lost the white queen," he said.

"Let me," said his great-niece, helping him to his feet and then stooping between the dark Edwardian chairs to find the missing piece. Amongst the chair drapes she felt the queen.

"Let's put her back where she belongs," said Uncle George. "You're only a powerful lady if you stay with the others," he rebuked.

Anna said, "I don't know, perhaps to break away from the rest is the most powerful thing she could do. Pure serendipity."

Duet

She concluded that she was lost; none of the road signs or features approximated the details Joy had given her. Her ambivalence about the whole enterprise increased as the uncertainty about where she was matched her own sense of belonging nowhere. Perhaps she had only come because Joy had been eager to give some help and Ellie had, in her weariness, agreed, not having the stamina to think of a good reason not to take up her offer. She wished that she was at home. At least there she wouldn't have been confronted by her own vulnerability as she was now. She drove on deciding that she must stop and ask directions as soon as she saw someone. That possibility looked less likely as the road narrowed and she realised there hadn't been a passing car for miles. Then a tractor approached.

She wound down the window and shouted to the young farm hand, "Can you tell me if I'm anywhere near Lane End Farm?"

"Mrs Rees' place? Yes, it's about two miles from here. Follow the road down to the minor crossroad and turn right. You can't miss it – look for the copse of trees. The trees that point to heaven," he said with a smile.

She thanked him and wondered whether his last remark was poetic or philosophic. The idea energised her for the last stage of her journey and the emptiness she had felt a few moments ago was replaced by a vague hopefulness that maybe this was a visit worth making.

She identified the trees easily; tall trees on a little knoll which indeed, against the fields which fell away from it, did seem to reach up to the sky, if not to heaven. Within minutes she had reached the farm and was carrying her bag to the cottage which stood beside it. Mrs Rees called a welcome and said that she would be across in a minute. Ellie opened the door, which led into a small sitting-room where a welcoming fire glowed. Although it was still warm outside, the coolness of a stone cottage would have been chilling without the gentle source of heat. She sat down and wondered whether this was the end or the beginning of her journey.

She closed her eyes and cut herself off from everything, and even rested for a while from her own thoughts. The silence was broken by a tap at the door. Mrs Rees appeared with a tray of tea.

"I thought you might like this after your journey. There's some salad in the fridge, and cheese and ham, if you want something to eat later on. I've left a list in the kitchen which I hope will help you find all you need, but give me a call if I can be of help. I expect for the moment you just want to rest."

Ellie thanked her with few words, not from ingratitude but from a wish not to get caught up in superficial conversation. Mrs Rees didn't seem like a woman who wanted that either. In fact, thought Ellie, as she drank the refreshing tea, she had either been well-primed by Joy or was a very sensitive woman. Which ever it was, it left Ellie with a hopeful sense of the possibilities for her stay in the country.

She slept well but awoke with a sense of heaviness. The journey yesterday had been diverting, if wearying, and her mind and emotions now flung her back into the blackness of the last few months and the exhaustion of the preceding years. The pain seemed very isolating. People who knew something of it were either embarrassed and studiously avoided it or pressurised Ellie to act as if none of these things had happened. So she carried it in her heart – a heart broken with anguish. The blackness seemed to shift her sense of time and it must have been almost midday before she went downstairs. There was some fresh milk on the table and a note from Mrs Rees – Lydia – inviting Ellie to join her on a walk with the dogs, later in the afternoon. The note communicated crisply all that needed to be said. Perhaps Ellie should make this a target for today, but she was still wary of people and the demands which might be made of her. She changed her mind a dozen times about the excursion with Lydia, but by the time it came to four o'clock she felt strong enough to undertake a stroll.

There was a warmth about Lydia that Ellie quickly became aware of. The walk was passed with an economy of words between companionable silences. Lydia took Ellie up to the copse of trees pointing to heaven. She talked about plants and animal movement in the trees with a true country woman's knowledge. She didn't press Ellie with questions but somehow seemed to know that she was deeply wounded. It felt strangely easy for Ellie to be with a woman she didn't know, who in saying little expressed a great deal about the still centre of being human. It was hard to analyse, and in fact Ellie didn't want to rob the feelings of their potency by doing just that. It was just good to experience.

The next few days passed with little contact between the women. Lydia was engaged with some farm business which took her into the neighbouring city on numerous occasions. Ellie slept and read, and as they were rainy days they allowed her the luxury of indulging in her rest without the more complex choices that would have arisen had she been tempted to go out. The cottage was a peaceful cocoon and food stocks were replenished each day before she awoke. Even at the moments when her mind took her back to the last years she could wander around her own memories with less of the searing anguish that usually occurred.

As the inner ache became soothed by the balm of silence and solitude Ellie became more alert to her surroundings. She began to observe the internal character of the cottage, savouring the atmosphere that was evoked by its timeless possessions. Even the sleepy ticking of the hall clock seemed to suggest that time was not an escaping commodity to be clutched at in desperation, but just another dimension punctuating each life story with sequential reference points. Ellie knew that part of what was aroused in her was the nostalgia of a city woman exploring the country. She smiled at this but decided she need not apologise, even to herself, for discovering that there can be a welcome hospitality in an atmosphere of peace and safety, even though that peace and safety had come from mental inventions of a sentimental kind.

If the inside of this cottage was Lydia's creation, Ellie decided that she was a woman of taste. For herself she was never sure how anyone could assemble furniture and pictures and ornaments to have unity without looking false, and to be casual without being untidy. But the cottage was a blend of wood and pottery, utensils and flowers, chintz and pictures which harmoniously sat amongst the healing green of field and tree. Ellie's eye wandered to this wider universe, and the calm of this haven began to permit some release from pain.

Ellie curled up on the sofa and wept bitter tears, which sprang from the pain of her body and soul. Somehow the energy of grief gave way to the stillness of sleep, and with Ellie's return to wakefulness came the heavy, but not unsatisfying sense of having allowed her body to feel what had been occluded by the need to care and the need to protect others from her hurt.

The slanting brightness of the sunset took Ellie to the window. She breathed deeply as if she had some new capacity to engage with the world. The surge of air in her lungs seemed to herald the beginnings of a fresh chapter in which she no longer needed to keep the world at bay but could allow her vulnerability to surface. As she relaxed into this newly discovered reality her eyes began to focus on the feathered stillness of a dead bird by the garden path. Only the angle of the evening sun served to distinguish the little body from the varied textures of nature, amongst which it might have lain unnoticed. Ellie looked at the tiny shape, resting forever from nature's purpose for it. She let out a sob. It seemed, in that moment, as if the bird was an unconscious symbol for all that had been lost in her life.

Lydia crossed the cottage lawn to the farm door. Her eyes alighted on the little bird and she stooped, picking it up gently. From the window Ellie saw the eyes and cupped hand of tenderness as Lydia held the bird while scooping the soft earth beneath the hedge in which to lay it. The private burial completed, Lydia stood pensively in the last light of day. Ellie watched, unnoticed, but knew that the gestures she had just witnessed possessed the unsentimental sensitivity to which one could entrust the pains of living.

The city business completed, Lydia returned to her farm routines. Distant but available to Ellie, she anticipated practical needs or appropriate moments for companionship.

"I'm planning on a long walk with the dogs tomorrow," Lydia said on Saturday evening. "They've missed their exercise while I've been away and so have I," she smiled. "Care to join us?"

"Love to," said Ellie without hesitation.

A sharp early-morning downpour freshened the earth, and the foliage basked in the warm sunshine which followed. Only a breeze which whispered and died, then to spring into flirtatious dance again, hinted at coolness. Ellie set out with Lydia and the dogs, freed for the first time in months – perhaps years – to feel there was no need to rehearse or anticipate what the day might bring. She did not have to decide on appropriate armour to conceal and protect. Their unhurried pace was punctuated by the more energetic double distances which the dogs covered in their freedom to flex sinew and muscle and explore the details of hedge and wood. Lydia took Ellie into a world of flora and fauna, which previously had only been an impressionistic backcloth of nature. She could not believe that what had previously passed as the still world of shrub-covered earth was a vibrant universe of throbbing life. Lydia had the sharp intellect of an educated woman combined with the humble scholar of the natural world; always alert to a new discovery but weaving it into her knowledge of science and art. Ellie was captivated by this refreshing human being whose supreme characteristic seemed a gentle peacefulness.

They trod paths previously unexplored by Ellie. Fresh perspectives on parts of the landscape which she was beginning to know and recognise caused gasps of delight as they opened up to her. She could not remember the last time the immediacy of experience had burst on her senses with such spontaneity and delight. She felt like a little girl again. The duet between discourse and silence evolved as naturally and soothingly as the ebb and flow of a calm incoming tide.

"Would you like a rest?" inquired Lydia. "I usually catch my breath and take in the view where the trees open up to the sky at the top of this path." Ellie recognised the trees pointing to heaven.

"I would like that very much," she said.

They sat on a grassy slope, Ellie already alert to the teeming universe.

"Nature can be both cruel and healing," said Lydia. It was an observation that arched between the ambiguity of the wooded dell and Ellie's grief.

"Could you bear it if I told you some of the cruelty of my experience?" asked Ellie.

"Of course," said Lydia quietly.

The tone of voice and meeting of eyes gave out a warmth, which instantly made the tears well in Ellie's eyes. As they ran uncontrollably down her cheeks and her body shook with its release from pain, Lydia moved close to her and put an arm around her shoulder, holding her hand with a firm but tender embrace of solidarity. Not since Paul had left her three years ago had Ellie found anyone whose concerns and opinions did not serve to stifle her own anguish. Here was a woman who simply held the pain without the need to prod or preach. As her emotion began to subside Ellie quietly told her story.

Paul's plausibility cost her many friends as she failed to communicate her own innocence in their social world; she the deserted wife, humiliated from years spent with a charming but philandering husband, he a man who eventually chose to expose and destroy an important but platonic relationship of Ellie's, as if she were the marriage wrecker. It still amazed her how easily truth could be less powerful than a convincing lie, especially one told to listeners whose preconceptions collude with the deceit. She had loved Paul. She always knew that her gift to him was complete devotion and his to her was a part-share in a phoney emotion, which he dressed up with poetic words of no substance. Ellie had lived with the compromise, somehow feeling that their unequal commitment was itself a chance to demonstrate the depth of what was in her heart.

"My son," she said to Lydia, "a carbon copy of his father, comes home sometimes, but is ill at ease with my intensity. Paul's charm and popularity are more persuasive than what I have to offer."

Lydia's concentration and gentle presence was not distracted by any other call on her attention. It served to reassure Ellie of her own human worth. Lydia had a picture of this loving woman being separated from all meaningful reference points and set adrift in a hostile sea. The story unfolded further, the intervening years had been taken up with the care of her father. He had always been her anchor point when things were hard, and he had been no less devoted and supportive at the end of her marriage. Just when a new pattern of security had been beginning to emerge, Ellie's father was told he had cancer. His illness was protracted and distressing. In the end Ellie undertook the burden of care, and watched his decline with a cumulative grief that tore at her heart. His death two months previously had been release from one agony and an emergence into a painful void.

"Joy said it would help coming here," said Ellie, as she stood outside her story for a moment and was able to offer some genuine, if inarticulate thanks to Lydia.

Lydia smiled and squeezed her hand. She was in no hurry and the power of Ellie sharing her experience became replaced by a no less potent silence in which the two women were bonded by the need of one and the care of the other. This human communion stood outside of time as each moved from personal reverie into awareness of the other with a depth of unspoken connection that Ellie had never before experienced.

As one who is freshly released from exhausting introspection, Ellie began to take in the green around her; the infinite variety of colour and shape and texture. It was as if she was awaking from a long sleep. A piercing shaft of light came through a gap in the trees overhead. Ellie looked into the light beyond the tall tree-trunks, and knew that this was the place given as a landmark when she had lost her way – 'The trees pointing to heaven.' Lydia saw a smile on Ellie's face, which for the first time was not a contradiction of what was going on inside.

"Tell me," Lydia said in a light and easy manner, half command, half question.

"Perhaps heaven is not up there but right here," Ellie said.

The two women looked wordlessly towards the sun as they gently embraced.

The Pink Straw Hat

Louisa-Jane walked down the road swinging her Woolworths carrier bag and singing a hymn to herself. She was on her way to a jumble sale at the Roman Catholic church. Her family were unfamiliar with the ways of Catholicism, being of evangelical inclination themselves, but a jumble sale, well that crossed all religious barriers. To Louisa-Jane it held untold fascination and the fact that this was the first time she was going to one alone gave an even greater thrill to her ten-year-old heart.

Her father had come from Jamaica some thirteen years previously at the time of the recruitment of West Indians by Birmingham City Transport. Her mother had arrived at a similar time to take up nursing. The meeting of the two was not so strange, after all they shared a common background and at times felt ill at ease in their new environment. Theirs was a good marriage. Her mother had given up her nursing when Louisa-Jane was born. Occasionally she would work at the General as a ward orderly, but not since the latest arrival two months ago. There were two boys between Lucy, the baby, and Louisa-Jane. They were aged five and six years and in common with other boys of that age, Nathan and Luke were a handful. This added to Louisa-Jane's sense of responsibility and already she was a little mother to the boys.

The current errand was a pleasant change from the shopping and tidying that had been her lot for the last two or three months. Her mother had given her thirty pence to spend on baby clothes and, if she saw one, a cardigan for herself. That was to be her eleventh birthday present.

She entered the church hall full of anticipation. Between the bobbing heads she could see trestle tables laden with clothes and household items. She made her way between two women who seemed to be looking at baby clothes. She thought that the pram suit for ten pence and the dress for five pence would be ideal and she knew that on these occasions she mustn't linger over her choice otherwise the opportunity would be lost. Holding them aloft she made a speedy transaction with a rather large, harassed lady and then put them into her carrier bag. If there was nothing else for Lucy she still had two bargains so she felt justified in edging along the table to cardigans. She was part way along when her progress was impeded by two women obviously vying for the same item in none-too-ladylike a fashion. Louisa-Jane took the opportunity to look at the stall. There in front of her was a pink straw hat. She picked it up with reverence. How long had she been wanting a pink hat for Sunday best? It had always been a kind of dream. "I can't manage it just now, dearie," her mother had said kindly, "one day you shall have one."

To Louisa-Jane the room might as well have become suddenly empty but for herself and the straw hat. It was a brighter pink where a ribbon had obviously once decorated its brim and a small hole at the base of the crown detracted from its former glory, if you were after a Paris creation, but to Louisa-Jane it was the most beautiful thing she had seen. She tried it on and even her mass of dark curls failed to stop it swinging round her head. 'A little big,' she thought, 'but that doesn't matter – it is really beautiful.' There was no mirror in which to judge her appearance but Louisa-Jane knew that this could be the culmination of a long ambition. But there was the cardigan and she knew that she had been able to come alone because her mother trusted her. She asked the price of the hat. It was ten pence. Well yes she could manage that, but perhaps she ought to pursue the cardigans. Maybe if she lingered they would all be gone and then she could buy the hat. She slowly made her way along the stall holding tightly to the hat. She kept it above the stall so as not to be thought stealing, and she watched as it glided over the chaos of clothes. It looked like a majestic liner making its way through the grey harbour. She arrived at cardigans and, without letting go of the hat, viewed with her carrier-bagged hand what there was for sale. There were several possibilities and in different circumstances the red one would have done admirably. But when you are ten and enchanted by a pink straw hat even a good sensible warm cardigan cannot make up. She stood for a moment and to her relief a thin woman with three sticky children bought it. That was one dilemma solved.

Louisa-Jane's mind was bursting with images of herself in that hat and while still entranced by her own day-dreams she handed over ten pence in payment. By this time things were being reduced and the lady with the thick glasses which slipped down her nose said that she could have it for six pence. With infinite relief she stood gazing about her, much to the annoyance of two young women with rather more practical business to pursue than a straw hat.

Louisa-Jane let herself be pushed to the back again and she fell to making some quick calculations. She still had nine pence and with that she thought she ought to make some retribution for the extravagance of the hat. With this thought in mind she pushed to the front and saw a box of socks. Now if anything would be useful it would be boys' socks. She made her selection of eight pairs at a penny each; one white pair and the others grey. Perhaps she could have the white ones and her brothers the others. She still had a penny left.

With a smile as wide as half a cheese she made her way to the door. She had made some practical choices, had fulfilled a long ambition and still had a penny change. If she had made her way there with excitement, she returned home with a joy that warmly filled every inch of her diminutive body. Surely her mother would approve of the expedition!

She tumbled into the kitchen where her mother was singing and feeding the baby. Louisa-Jane knew the order in which she must produce the items and so, like a magician achieving calculated effect on his audience, she started by rooting to the bottom of her bag for the baby clothes. She watched her mother closely to assess the response. They both laughed gaily as she held the items beside the feeding child

"A little big but they are beautiful," reassured her mother, who leant over to hug her daughter, nearly suffocating the baby in the process. They laughed again. Louisa-Jane felt into the bag once more and carefully detected the woolliness of the grey socks.

"I thought these would be good for Nathan and Luke," she said, in a voice her mother would have used when picking up a bargain. "And now," she said, lingering over the words as she found the white socks nestling inside the hat, "these are for me."

"Good," said her mother, "and a cardigan?" This was more difficult and Louisa-Jane knew that what happened in the next few minutes would either confirm her joy or bring anguish, if her special purchase brought disapproval.

"Well there wasn't anything quite my size." Louisa-Jane hedged round the truth, feeling a pounding guilt in her heart for preparing a deceitful route to her extravagance.

"Never mind," said her mother, "you've done very well. Any change?"

"Yes," said Louisa-Jane, holding out the penny.

"Well keep that, dearie, for being such a good help to me." The noisy suckling of the child and the kindness of her mother gave Louisa-Jane some confidence for her confession.

"No," she said, "you can have the penny back because I did get something else at the jumble sale." She opened the carrier bag and pulled the hat from its hiding place. She was already familiar with its shape and texture, having taken great care to extricate the items of clothing without damaging the precious millinery. Her eyes were fixed on her mother's face.

"Oh, is that for me?" she laughed, "Your dad will say, 'Just look at you, what a dazzler!'" She momentarily dislodged the feeding baby as she perched the hat on her head.

Re-establishing contact with the protesting child gave Louisa-Jane an unseen moment to wipe the moisture from her eye. Was her prize really lost to her mother? She looked at her warm, loving parent, who was surely the best person in the whole world, and knew with the certainty of all those ingrained Sunday School stories that to claim the hat as her own would be a sin of selfishness of the highest order. She knew that Jesus would never withhold a pink straw hat from someone who so clearly wanted it. She felt, without knowing what it was, a devastating disappointment, which could not be shared, clutch her throat enough to choke her.

At that moment the boys appeared. They looked at their mother, rocking the satisfied baby with the hat gradually slipping to the back of her head. Luke pointed and they both began to laugh. Soon Louisa-Jane joined in, glad to give vent to some emotion, even if it wasn't what she was feeling most strongly. They all rocked with uncontrolled and self-generating laughter which spilled into tears and holding stomachs and altogether seemed to end in a quite different place from where it had begun. As the merriment subsided Louisa-Jane felt again the stab of loss.

"It isn't mine," said her mother to the boys, "I was just teasing Lou. It's hers really."

Louisa-Jane took the hat with one hand and hugged her mother with the other, with all the joy and relief that might follow an averted disaster. The boys looked as she put it on. She could see their attentive eyes behind her as she looked in the kitchen mirror.

"You look lovely," her mother said and the boys grinned because they hadn't learned to say grown-up things to their sister.

A piece of white ribbon had been found to adorn the brim and by swirling it into a little posy the hole had been covered. Louisa-Jane walked into church feeling so happy that even the faded green dress could not detract from the poise she felt within herself. She sat between her mother and father. If she tilted her eyes as far up as she could, she could just see the brim of her pink hat. Occasionally she raised a tentative hand to touch the side of the hat, both for the comfort of feeling it and to ensure it sat at the right angle. She almost lost it when she turned suddenly to stare at some giggling boys behind her. Louisa-Jane suspected that they were laughing at her (maybe even her hat), but she felt a superior sense of security that could not be touched by infantile mockery.

"Let us pray," said the preacher.

Louisa-Jane knew that the preoccupation with the hat had quite obliterated her sense of devotion. She remembered the preacher who had told the congregation about pride and thinking too highly of yourself. For a moment the memory sent a cloud scudding over the sunny joy that filled her heart. For a moment she wished she had bought the cardigan and not the hat and maybe she would not have risked the mortal dangers of vanity. The voice of the preacher penetrated her reverie.

"We thank you, good Lord for all those unexpected joys which lighten our lives."

"Amen," echoed the voices of the congregation. 'He means my hat,' thought Louisa-Jane, 'that is an unexpected joy which has lightened my life.' She relaxed, feeling that wherever the good Lord was, he would surely really approve of the hat and maybe, like the missionary who had seen so many signs of the good Lord in everyday life, perhaps it had been put there by God, for her. The thought was so liberating that Louisa-Jane said 'Amen' under her breath and like some of the old men at the back of the church she held up her hands and said for everyone to hear,

"Thank you, Lord." Her mother turned and smiled and it seemed as if the whole of the universe approved of the pink straw hat.